MW01145861

I

J.B. Sensenbrenner

II

CRACKED SIDEWALKS

A New Orleans Mystery

By

J.B. SENSENBRENNER

CRACKED SIDEWALKS

A New Orleans Mystery

By

By J.B. Sensenbrenner

This work of fiction is dedicated to my wife Carol who inspired me to write about her favorite place to be. She truly loves New Orleans and all it's about. She loves the people, the food and the music.

The author wants to thank... Amy "Amis" Skinner for her high energy and insightful editing work; authors Erica Spindler, Susan Fleet, and Joe Formichella for their encouragement at the Tennessee Williams Masters Classes; Authors George Sanchez, Mikko Machionne and Adrian Martin for their insightful comments and suggestions; Nadra Enzie for his inspiration of what a hero really is; Frank Krommer for his never ending technical support; and thank you Debbie, Mike, Mary, Robb, Carl, Henry, Lori, Phyllis, Roger, Cindy, Bill, Wayne, Terrell, Susan, Frank, Diane, John, Paul, Rocco, Janice, Chuck, James, Kelly, Peter, Jane, Bob, Caryl, Brian, Mary B. Mike, Tom, Susie, Jason, Csaba, David, Connie, Charlie, Amanda, Frank, Darrel, Lucas, Anthony, Lawrence, George, Ed, and Jennifer. Thank you for your love, kindness and friendship.

J.B. Sensenbrenner

VIII

"I think New Orleans is such a beautiful city. It looks like a fairy tale when you walk through the French Quarter or the Garden District. There is such a lush sense of color, style, architecture – and the people themselves."
Anikia Noni Rose

"New Orleans is unlike any city in America. Its cultural diversity is woven into the food, the music, the architecture. It's a sensory experience on all levels and there's a story lurking on every corner."
Rita Sepetys

"I've been all over the world. I love New York, Paris, San Francisco, so many places. But there's no place like New Orleans. It's got the best food. It's got the best music. It's got the best people. It's got the most fun stuff to do."
Harry Connick, Jr.

IX

*"We dance even if there's no radio.
We drink at funerals. We talk too
Much and laugh too loud & live too large and,
frankly, we're suspicious of others who don't."*
Chris Rose

*"I'm New Orleans born, New Orleans bred, and
when I die, I'll be New Orleans dead."*
Paul Sanchez

*"Behind every man now alive stand 30 ghosts, for
that is the ratio by which the dead outnumber the
living."*
Arthur C. Clarke

Chapter 1

New Orleans, Louisiana
Monday, January 7ᵗʰ

The sound of a thousand drums rumbled outside as if the Roman army led by Augustus Caesar was invading. The drums rumbling and chariots racing grew louder and more intimidating in the darkness. Arrows in the form of lightning bolts soared from the heavens. Perhaps God was angry at us mortals for our carefree and sinful ways.

More rumbling, louder, in opposite directions made it seem that we're surrounded by different armies caught in a terrible conflict, not knowing who is fighting or what is the prize?

With such madness going on we hunker down waiting for it to end. But, it goes on and on with loud thunder and terrifying lightning strikes cracking closer, shaking our humble dwelling.

Finally, the dark sky collapses, overloaded with water, pouring it down to extinguish the battle, flooding the fields, streets and walkways.

Then, there's silence. The thunder, lightning and rain ceased as if they were nothing but a figment of the imagination or just a dream of power, might and wonder.

The front door squeaked open and the sweet fragrance of outside air rushed in. It was so invigorating that I inhaled deeply filling my lungs. I walked over to close the door, found my wife Carlotta outside standing on the stoop, arms extended, head back with her open mouth sucking in the fresh air.

She sensed me watching and slowly turned around, and smiled. "Isn't it amazing?"

I wrapped my arms around her in agreement and squeezed her tight.

She let out a big sigh and said "Let's go for a walk."

"No. Let's go inside. It might rain again."

She inhaled deeply and purred "the air smells so fresh. Let's go for a walk."

"No. It's late."

She pushed my arms off. "We can take umbrellas."

"No. I don't wanna go."

"You're no fun. I'll go alone."

"No. It's not safe for a woman to walk alone at night."

"I've done it before."

"Come on in," I insisted and turned around to walk into the house. She didn't follow me. I walked back out and saw her walking away and shouted "CARLOTTA, PLEASE COME BACK."

I watched her vanish in the darkness. She didn't come back.

2:00 AM, Tuesday

Bruce wakes up to screaming sirens and reaches over to the left side of the bed to feel… nothing. She's not there. He sits up, flicks the switch on the light on the night stand. Her side of the bed's still made. He jumps up and walks out into the kitchen and living room. She's not there. He checks his cell phone for calls or texts. Nothing.

He takes a deep breath. *What should I do?* He sits down in the living room. *She'll be home any minute.* After a few minutes, he thinks *I can't just sit here. I've got to find her.* He pulls a hoodie over his shirt and walks out into the darkness to look for her.

She had gone out alone before, but always came back well before midnight. He walks faster and faster as thoughts circle his mind. Where is she? *Is she in trouble? Is she hurt? It's not like her to stay out this late. Something's wrong. Oh my God. I hope nothing's happened to her. I should have gone with her.*

When he turns the corner on Royal Street he sees people standing outside a late night restaurant smoking. He walks into d.b.a. and sees people dancing to the music of a brass band of trumpets and trombones playing New Orleans jazz. He leans over the bar and asks the bartender if she's seen Carlotta. She nods "yes" and tells him that she saw her earlier. The bartender walks away to serve another customer.

Bruce walks across the street to the Spotted Cat. A band is playing in the stage by the front window. He asks the bartender if she's seen a woman with short brown hair wearing a denim jacket and black shirt. "Honey, there's a lot of people that look like that."

He looks in the other clubs that were open. No one's seen her. He walks back at 3:00 AM, stopping at each corner to look for her down the side streets. He sees a couple embracing on the corner of the R-Bar. The woman has short brown hair and is wearing a denim jacket. He walks across the street and coughs to get their attention. They break up and turn around to look at him. It isn't her. The guy yells "What's your problem asshole?"

He walks down Esplanade and sees several people sitting, drinking and laughing on the neutral ground (which are medians, but called "neutral grounds" in New Orleans because they divided different cultures when the city was developed three hundred years ago). He quickly looks away knowing that she wouldn't be there. As he approaches the corner of Burgundy and

4

Esplanade he hears people talking in the front bar at Buffa's. He walks in and sees a dozen people sitting and standing at the bar, *but not her*. He asks the bartender if he's seen her. He says that the last time he saw her was when she was with Bruce on Friday night,

Bruce walks home dejected. *Knowing something's wrong. Seriously wrong.* As he opens the front door, he feels a warm sensation of optimism that she would be lying in bed. *But she's not there.*

J.B. Sensenbrenner

Chapter 2

Six months later, Bruce is a broken man
10:00 AM, Monday, July 8th

I tripped and fell on Barracks Street. I should've been watching my step but instead was looking at the old shotgun houses across the street. *Carlotta loved the simple design of those houses.* I had walked daily since she left. I still didn't know what happened to her. I stood up and brushed the bits of gravel and leaves off my hands and scraped knee. I think how little *the knee hurts compared to the deep pain burning inside about losing her. I should've walked with her that night. It's my fault. Nothing would've happened if I'd gone out with her.*

There's fighting inside one of the houses across the street. A man's yelling. A woman's screaming and crying. Furniture's breaking. Things banging on walls. Then there's silence.

I looked around to see if anyone else heard the commotion. Just as I was about to walk away, the front door burst open and a big, burly man tumbles down the stoop, growling like a bear. He gets up as fast as he fell and runs out of sight around the corner.

I froze, as my brain tried to process what happened. The door was left wide open. So was my mouth. After waiting a few minutes to see if the guy was coming back, I walked across the street and looked inside at a body lying on the old wood floor. She wasn't moving. I took a deep breath, knelt down on one knee and rolled her over on her back. Her throat was black with bruises. I felt relieved that it wasn't Carlotta.

I held her wrist but couldn't feel a pulse, so I leaned forward to place my ear by her mouth to see if I could feel any air and to see if I could notice the rise and fall of her chest from breathing. Nothing. I gently lifted her head, but her neck felt like jelly. Her neck was broken. I carefully set her head down. *She's dead*.

She looked to be in her late twenties with auburn hair and fair skin. She wore a light pink tank top with tattered blue jean shorts. She was barefoot. Her toe nails were painted pink. I dug my cell phone out of my pocket and called 911.

I heard people talking outside on the sidewalk and saw them looking at me. It made me feel uncomfortable, so I walked out, closed the door and sat on the stoop to wait for the police.

When they arrived with blue lights flashing, I stood up and waved to get their attention. Two officers got out of their car and walked up to me. I told them what happened, and they walked into the house. An officer held his radio up and called for an ambulance. Twenty minutes later it pulled up, red lights flashing. Minutes later, a second squad car pulled up on the corner. Officers order the gathering crowd to stand back.

I told the detectives that came in the second car what I'd seen. They radio their dispatch to alert other units that the killer's on foot in the Quarter. It made me think of the crime shows on TV. Only this was for real. And, I was in the middle of it as the key witness.

***

A couple hours later, I sat down on an empty wrought iron bench facing the St. Louis Cathedral by Jackson Square. I was shook up thinking about what happened. I was perspiring from the walk and started panting and coughing. I couldn't get enough air. I felt like I was stuck in a bad dream within a bad dream. I hadn't slept in over six months because of worrying about Carlotta. *And how guilty I felt for not walking with her that night. Because of me, she's missing. Maybe dead. Now, I witnessed a murder of a woman. Maybe that's what happened to Carlotta.*

Then I saw him. The murderer. He was wearing a dark blue bandana over his head. He was sitting three benches down talking to two tough looking guys who were covered with tattoos. In fact, there was so much ink on their arms and necks, that it was difficult to see skin. They were smoking and talking loudly. The burly guy was talking with his arms swinging in the air. Tourists walking by sped up when they heard their foul language. When the killer looked my way, I dropped my head to avoid eye contact. Although I was trembling, I managed to stand up and walk towards Muriel's Restaurant on the corner. When they were out of sight, I called 911.

The woman that answered seemed clueless. Maybe it was my fault because I was stammering so much. I crouched down and cupped the phone so no one else could hear. I told her that the Barracks Street killer is sitting on a bench in front of the St. Louis Cathedral. I spelled out my name and explained that I had called in a couple hours earlier to report the murder. She asked for my location and made me repeat why I was calling again. I lost my patience after telling her loud and clear that the killer was sitting on a goddam bench in front of the St. Louis Cathedral and hung up.

***

About 20 minutes later, two police cars pulled up. Four officers dressed in blue shirts and white helmets got out and walked towards the benches. Swear to God, just about everyone sitting on benches got up and walked away in a mass exodus. It made me wonder if they were illegal immigrants, wanted criminals or just nervous tourists.

The empty benches made it easy for the officers to spot him. As the officers approached, the killer stood up and started shouting profanities at them. He punched the closest officer and started to run, but a second officer tackled him and knelt on his back, while a third officer pulled his arms behind his back and cuffed him. The two men who were sitting with him didn't resist. They raised their hands in the air. The officers screamed at the men to get down. With guns pointed at them, they dropped to the ground. The officers cuffed them and pulled them up on their feet. They searched their pockets and removed three small hand guns, two switchblades, brass knuckles, their wallets and cell phones.

Another squad car arrived and two more officers ran over to help. The men were loaded one at a time into the back seats of the three squad cars.

Several tourists actually moved closer to take pictures. More people gathered to watch what was going on thinking that it was a scene being filmed for a TV show or movie. *Except there were no cameras*.

An officer recognized me standing by the corner of the cathedral. He was one of the officers who had been at the Barracks Street crime scene two

11

hours earlier. I told him that the killer was the guy with the dark blue bandana.

As the police cars drove away, the killer turned around to look out the rear window. He saw me talking to the officer. *I felt like a marked man.*

Chapter 3

8:15 AM, Tuesday, July 9th

The phone buzzes. It surprised me since I hardly ever receive calls. I mostly get emails and text messages.

"Hello."

"This is Detective Joe Rank of the NOPD. Is this Bruce Paul?"

"Yes. I'm Bruce Paul."

"We want to talk to you. Can you come down to the police station on Royal Street?"

"Yes, I can be there at 9:00 AM."

"Thank you, Mr. Paul."

I put on my sneakers, locked the door and walked down Esplanade to Royal Street. I started to worry as I walked about being involved in a murder case.

I walk past a group of people milling around on the neutral ground

People were sitting, standing, squatting and lying down. Most of them wore brown colored clothing. Locals called them "gutter punks" or

13

"train hoppers" because they rode in on the rails, didn't work and begged for money and left over carry out food. They were usually harmless with the exception of when they had too much to drink or were drugged up. Their aggressive pan handling, sitting and laying in shop entry ways were nuisances that the police somehow ignored until someone got hurt.

I crossed the street and walked past the house of an old friend who was sitting on his front porch strumming Dixie on a cigar box guitar. We exchanged high waves and smiles.

I'm walking fast with my head down so I don't trip on the cracked sidewalks and don't see the killer's friends standing on the next corner until it's too late. I walk out on the street to avoid them, but, they step out too.

"How ya doing?"

One of them grunts back, "Not too fucking good." He grabs my arm and pulls me over to the curb. "Where the fuck do you think you're going?"

"Hey, let go."

The other guy punches me in the stomach. It felt like his fist went through me. I hunched over in pain. Then, I was hit on the back of the head, knocking me down on the sidewalk. Instinctively I curled up in a fetal position with my arms in front of my face to protect myself. They took turns kicking me from both sides again and again and again.

When I regained consciousness I see legs and shoes and hear voices, but, can't understand what's being said. After a few minutes, my head clears a little and I hear someone saying "he's disgusting." Another says "he's a junkie or just a drunk." People spit on me. Somebody tosses pennies. I sit up when a dog pees on my head.

I ached so much that I couldn't think straight. *Maybe they're right that I'm disgusting and don't deserve to live. My wife's missing. I couldn't protect her. Why should I live? Maybe I'm better off dead. I should've gone out with her. She'd be alive if I did.*

My mouth tastes salty and gritty. I feel numb and cold. Cold all over. So cold that when I try to stand up, I fall back down. It's as if I've been run over by a truck. I'm dizzy and light headed. Finally, I'm able to stand. *I'm late for my meeting at the police station. I have to get there.*

I walk away slowly. People are moving out of my way. It feels like I'm walking through them.

***

I made it to the police station and told the receptionist that I was late for a meeting with Detective Rank. I was told to sit down while they called him. A few minutes later Rank introduced himself as the lead investigator on the case.

"Mr. Paul, please call me Joe," Rank said.

15

Joe was tall with wavy brown hair and a handle bar mustache. He looked like he was out of the old west. He wore a shoulder holster and a badge on his belt.

After shaking hands, he walked me down the hall into a small office with an old gray military style desk and asked me to sit down in an old wood chair.

"Coffee, soda or water?" He offered.

"Just water."

After handing me a plastic bottle of water, Rank said, "Thank you for coming down on such short notice." *But, I'm late because of the beating. Why doesn't he ask me why I'm late?'*

"Where did you shoot that buck?" I asked looking up at 12 point buck mounted on the wall behind Rank.

"I shot him two years ago near Stanley, Mississippi. We called him Halo, because we had field camera pictures of him on a sunny July day when he was in velvet."

"He's a beautiful buck, that's for sure."

"Do you hunt?"

"I used to hunt years ago. It was a great way to spend time with my friends and sons. We had a lot of fun working on food plots and trails in the woods."

I looked over at a large painting of an old plantation house on the side wall. Rank watched me and said "that's an old sugar plantation out in the country. Life was a lot slower back then. Some people think it was better."

I wasn't sure what he meant by *better?* I had goose bumps. "Can you turn down the air conditioning? I'm freezing. I rubbed my arms.

"I wish we had air conditioning but this old building is only equipped with ceiling fans, but as you can see, there isn't one here. Mr. Paul, first of all, let me thank you for finding the murder suspect. Thanks to you he's in custody."

He stared at me and added, "I understand that your timing was flawless. You just happened to be walking by when the murder occurred. And a couple hours later you find the guy by Jackson Square."

Rank smiled and waved his hand over the foot high stacks of papers and files on his desk and said "I wish all our cases were solved so quickly."

I nodded. "I was just walking by the house, minding my own business when it happened." *I feel dizzy and have trouble focusing on Rank.*

"Well, Mr. Paul, you're the key witness. You're the only witness that puts the suspect at the murder scene." His words stuck me like a dart. *I thought about the killer looking at me from the back seat of the squad car.*

"Please. Call me Bruce."

"Will do Bruce. What do you do for a living?"

"I'm a writer. I write short stories, songs, poems and novels."

17

"Bruce, if it's okay with you, I want to record your testimony."

"No problem."

He set his cell phone on the desk and touches the button to start the audio recording. He asks me to start at the beginning and tell him what happened.

"It was about 10:00 AM on Monday, July 8th, when I left my house on Esplanade to walk to Jackson Square. I walk every day, sometimes earlier, sometimes later, ever since my wife left." I bowed my head and paused as I squeezed my lips to control myself from breaking up.

"Sorry."

"No problem. It's a real tragedy that your wife was never found. Although I didn't work on it since it was a 'missing person' and not a 'murder case,' I was aware that she was never found. It's gotta be tough for you not knowing. I hope you get closure soon."

I started again. "I was walking down Barracks Street. It was quiet. I didn't see any other people out. I tripped and fell down on the cracked sidewalks when I heard people fighting in a shotgun house across the street. My wife loved the simple design of the shotgun houses." I squeezed my lips together again.

"Sorry... I heard a man yelling and a woman screaming and crying and loud pounding and banging, like on the walls. Then everything was

18

quiet. A few minutes went by and I was about to walk away when the front door burst open. A guy wearing a black leather vest, blue bandana, and heavily tattooed arms tumbled down the stoop, growling like a bear. He got up as fast as he fell and ran around the corner. He left the door wide open.

After waiting a few minutes to see if he was returning, I walked across the street and looked inside. I saw a body lying on the floor. I went inside to see if I could help. It was a woman. I turned her over on her back and knelt down to check her breathing and pulse. There was none. I called 911 and waited for the police to come. The killer never returned."

I looked up. "It happened so fast."

Rank said, "Did you get a good look at the guy?"

"Yes. I'll never forget him. It was like he was shot out of a cannon. He burst out the door, fell down, got up and ran away."

"Was there anyone else in the house?"

"No. I didn't see or hear anyone else."

"Anything more?"

"No. It happened so fast. That's it. Well, wait a minute there's more. After the police told me I could go, I walked down to Jackson Square and sat down on a bench in front of the Cathedral. It was crowded with tourists but I saw the killer sitting on a bench talking to two other guys."

"And, that's when you called the police station a second time?"

"Yes. But first I walked away, out of the killer's sight, and called 911. It must have been about twelve noon. About twenty minutes later two police cars pulled up and the officers arrested the killer and his friends."

"Okay. Is there anything else?"

I took a deep breath. "Yeah. The killer saw me. He saw me talking to one of the police officers as he rode away."

When I was done, Rank turned off the recording and told me that he wanted me to identify the man in a line up. He explained how it worked. It was just like on TV. He said if I didn't mind waiting a bit they could put together the line up right away and save me a trip from coming back.

I was surprised they (NOPD) could move that fast.

Rank told me to sit tight and left me in his office. About twenty minutes later he came back and asked me to follow him down the hall into a room with several folded chairs set up in a row facing a large window.

"Please sit."

Rank leaned forward to speak into a microphone "Ready, Sargent."

Five men walked out and stood facing us behind the glass. It was eerie as they stood looking around. They were only ten feet away but couldn't see us.

The men were dressed alike. Rank ordered the first man to step forward. He was rough looking, unshaven, tattoos but was not the killer. The same process continued until it got to number four. When asked, he took two steps forward. I had recognized him when they first walked out. "It's number four, Number four. He's the guy I saw run out of the house." I whispered.

"Are you sure? Are you really sure?" Rank spoke in a normal voice.

"Yes. I'm positive it's number four."

"Thank you."

I was shaking when leaving the room, following Rank back to his office. Gripping both arms on the chair I asked "Was there any way they could see us?"

"No. It's a one way mirror. We can see them but they can't see us."

"Could they hear us?"

"No. It's sound proof glass."

"Any other questions?"

"When's the trial?"

"You'll be notified when the trial's scheduled. We want you to stay in New Orleans so you're available when needed." He handed me his card and said to call if I have any more questions. He stood up and reached out his hand, "Thanks again for your help." He walked me out of his office into the hall way and pointed towards the exit door.

***

When I opened the door to leave, I saw the two thugs sitting on the steps. They stood when they saw me. Immediately I turned around and walked back into the station and up to the police officer at the desk. "I've got a problem. There are two guys outside who are friends of the murderer."

Rank must've overheard me as he walked over and asked, "What's the problem?"

I point at the front door. "The killer's buddies are outside."

Rank walked over to the front door and looked outside but didn't see anyone. He walked back and said "Come with me."

I followed him out a side door into the parking lot. He told me to get into an unmarked car and drove me home. He explained that those guys should've been held longer, but, they were released on bail the same day. He told me to call if they give me any problems.

"Stay safe," he said, before driving away.

Chapter 4

6:00 AM, Thursday, July 11th

I woke up staring at the bedroom ceiling, listening to sirens screaming by. I felt like a prisoner because I was afraid to leave the house for fear of being murdered by the killer's friends.

After staying inside for three days, I wasn't only stir crazy, but hungry because the refrigerator was empty. I waited for daylight before dressing in a hoodie, baseball cap, khaki shorts and sunglasses to blend in and not stand out in any way. I cracked open the door and looked both ways before venturing out. All clear.

My neighbor Leo was sitting on his stoop taking a long drag on a cigarette.

"How ya doin' Leo?

"Doin', just doin'."

"Anything goin' on the street?"

"No. Nothin'. Same O, same O."

"Well, have a good one."

My grocery shopping was limited to the number of bags I could carry for twelve blocks back home. So I prioritized it. First, I bought a twelve pack of Abita Amber, next a frozen pizza, sliced luncheon meat, bread, eggs, bananas, peanut butter, strawberry jam, peanuts, and chocolate covered almonds. I was a completely different shopper than my wife, who was a gourmet cook and "too good" of a shopper (because she would cruise down every aisle carefully looking over every item, making me wait forever it seemed in the car). *But she was missing.*

Chapter 5

12:00 PM

When I got back home, I saw a white-bearded man sitting on my stoop. He was sleeping with his head down. I walked past him carrying four bags of groceries and closed the door softly not to disturb him.

It felt good to get out and felt even better to eat a peanut butter and jelly sandwich. I washed it down with a cold beer. I put the rest of the groceries away and felt so good that I called an old friend, Rocky, and asked him to meet me at 3:00 PM at Pat O'Brien's.

***

I arrived first and sat down at an empty table by the rear wall so I could watch people coming and going. I ordered a Hurricane, but told the waiter, dressed neatly in a green top coat with white pants, to keep the tab open as a friend would be joining me shortly.

On cue, Rocky, wearing a black Ben Hogan cap backwards, sunglasses and chewing on a stubby cigar, walked in like he owned the place. He pushed the waiter who greeted him out of his way and walked towards me.

"Hey Rocky."

"Long time, no see. What've you been up to? You been out of town or just laying low?"

"I haven't been going out. Ever since Carlotta left, I haven't gone out much, only to the grocery store. This is the first time in more than six months that I've been in a bar."

"Ya, I haven't seen you around. Figured you were laying low because of your wife missing. You've had it rough. I've felt bad for you, man. Can't believe they never found her."

The waiter interrupted us by setting a hurricane in front of Rocky. He took a long sip and looked up at me. "Hey, it's good to see you. So, what's the scoop? Is it about your wife? Did the police find out what happened to her?"

"No. I think the police have given up. I can't quit thinking about her. How can a person vanish into thin air? I don't know if the police are even working on it anymore. I don't hear from them."

"I hate to say it but are you sure she wasn't fooling around with some other guy and ran off with him?"

"No. No, she'd never do that. We were having fun together." I looked away feeling frustrated.

26

Rocky tapped his straw and took another sip. "Sorry, I didn't mean to upset you. So what'd you wanna talk about?"

I looked left and right and said in a low voice to make sure no one else could hear. "I witnessed a murder."

Rocky started coughing. I waited for him to quit and then told him what happened.

"Ye Gods! So let me get this straight. You were walking down Barracks Street at mid-morning four days ago, heard a couple fighting, found a body and saw the guy who did it. Is that right?"

"Yeah. And I was the only person on the street that saw him. There was nobody else around. That part of Barracks is residential, so there weren't any tourists walking by at the time. A short time later I spotted the killer sitting on a bench in front of Jackson Square. I called 911 to report it. The police arrested him.

"The next day I was beat up and left to die by the killer's buddies on my way to the police station. I thought I was dead, but somehow, I walked to the station and identified him in a police lineup as the murderer. The police told me that I should not leave the city until the trial's over."

Rocky shook his head. "Geezus. If I were you, I'd be really worried. You're between a rock and a hard place. You're screwed. Christ, first your wife's missing and now you're involved in a murder.

Your life is going from bad to worse. " He looked at me and moved his cigar around his mouth.

Then he added, "Hey, the killer and his goons don't know where you live, right? And they don't know your name, right? If I were you, I'd call the police to ask if there's any way that they know your name or address. For Christ's sake you don't want your identity published in the paper or anywhere else."

Chapter 6

9:00 PM

After sunset, a young woman wearing tight gold shorts and a revealing midi strolled down Esplanade. She stopped on the corner in front of Buffa's, lit a cigarette under the street light and slowly looked left and right. She inhaled deeply and blew out a long puff of smoke. She saw Leo sitting on his stoop wearing a white tank top and old plaid shorts, holding a bottle of beer, watching her. She walked over to him. I couldn't hear what was being said, but could guess as she spoke to him with one leg on his stoop. She had a pretty smile. The kind of smile that makes men melt. Without looking back, Leo held her hand and led her inside.

A few hours later, that same night, my friend Dave walked down the middle of the neutral ground toward the small corner liquor store. A young boy with orange tipped dreadlocks walked up to him, pulled out a gun and pointed it at his chest and said in a soft voice "Give me what you got."

Dave was easily twice the size of the young robber. He was "street smart" from 17 years of bartending in New York City's Time Square. He wore a concealed weapon under his jacket. He looked at the youth and then down at the gun pointed at his chest.

Dave called at 12:30 AM and told me what happened.

"Hey Bruce. I hope I'm not waking you up."

"No, what's going on?"

"I just got held up."

"Oh my God. What happened?" I sat up on the bed.

"I was walking to that small corner liquor store to buy cigarettes, when this young kid walks up and points a gun at my chest. He said in a soft voice, 'Give me what ya got.' Two thoughts flashed through my mind real fast. Although I had my concealed carry gun on my back, I thought that I'd probably miss the kid if I shot because he was so thin, and secondly, I could see the headlines in the *Times Picayune* the next morning 'MAN SHOOTS TEENAGER!'"

Dave added, "What seemed odd was that the kid's gun had an orange tip on the end of the barrel. It happened so fast. The gun might have been a toy. But, I thought what if it's real?"

Dave said he decided not to reach for his weapon but instead pulled his wallet out of his back pocket and dropped it on the ground. The kid picked it up and ran across the street. There was another kid and the two of them ran out of sight past the liquor store. There was no cash in the wallet. Dave had planned to use the ATM machine at the store to withdraw cash to buy cigarettes. Instead he turned around and walked home to call his bank to report the stolen debit card.

"Are you OK? Is there anything I can do to help, Dave?"

He chuckled and added, "No. I'm OK. It just happened so fast. I wasn't expecting it. The kid appeared out of nowhere. I only had a few seconds to react... whether to resist by grabbing his gun, or pull my gun out or just give him my empty wallet. I dropped my wallet on the ground.

He picked it up and ran across the street out of sight.

The kid must've been no older than 14. It's funny when I think about it now that his orange tipped dreadlocks and orange tipped gun barrel kinda matched. I wonder if the gun was real or a toy."

"Are you gonna report it to the police?"

"Yeah. I'll call them now." Then he added, "Just take care yourself. It's the wild west out there."

I couldn't sleep after hanging up the phone. I stepped outside for some fresh air and thought about what Dave said "how it happened so fast. That the kid appeared out of nowhere." I looked carefully at the neutral ground and spotted a dead cat lying in a pile of leaves. I walked over to look at it more closely. When I knelt down to touch the cat, it turned its head and snarled. I jumped back in surprise as the cat stood up, arched its back and walked away snarling.

As I walked back across the street, Leo opened his door to let the young woman out. She turned around to kiss him and walked away towards Buffa's. She stopped in the same spot on the corner and lit a cigarette under the street light. Leo yawned and shut his door.

Chapter 7

7:00 AM, Friday, July 12th

I woke up the next morning when I could see sunlight leaking through the wood shutters. I walked into the living room and cracked them open just enough to peak outside. Two men jogged by in dark blue gym trunks and white t-shirts.

I recognized them and opened the door to yell out "Hey Donnie. Hey Marcell!" They were good friends who owned a beautiful Bed & Breakfast mansion on Marigny Street. Donnie was an outstanding writer who wrote two novels that were set in New Orleans.

The white-bearded man was sitting on the stoop. I didn't see him at first. He was becoming a fixture. Kinda like having a live-in gnome.

Although the sidewalk was dry, the street was wet which meant the city had already done its job of sweeping and washing the streets. It always amazed me how the city worked so hard to clean up the mess left over from tourists the night before. Why are people so messy tossing litter, plastic glasses, bottles and paper on the sidewalks and streets?

I shuffled my shoeless feet to the kitchen island bar and sat down to look at my lap top computer. I started checking my email. It was mostly junk mail.

I called up the NOPD. "Hello, can I speak to Detective Rank?"

"Just a minute."

"Hello. This is Detective Rank."

"Hi Joe. This is Bruce Paul. I have a question."

"Yes, Mr. Paul. What's your question?"

"Bruce. Please call me Bruce."

"What's your question?"

"Does the killer's attorney know my name and address?"

"No Sir. We don't give out names or addresses."

"Is there any way that he'll learn my name and address from the media?"

"No Sir. The media will not have access to that information until after the trial." Then he added, "His attorney will know who you are because we have to share our evidence and witnesses with him. It's part of the trial protocol."

"Oh, boy. That's a big problem. I 'm worried that they'll try to kill me to prevent me from testifying. Is there any way you can withhold my identity until the trial?"

"I'll contact the DA immediately and tell him you've been threatened, and you requested anonymity."

34

***

I heard an argument outside my door and opened it to see Rocky fighting with the white-bearded guy sitting on the stoop.

"Who in the hell is this guy? I tried to knock on your door and he grabbed me."

I told the white-bearded guy. "It's OK. Rocky's a friend".

He released him. Rocky growled at him as he brushed off his shirt and walked into the house.

He sat down in my favorite lazy boy chair before I could, wiped the sweat off his brow with a wrinkled handkerchief and said "Who's that crazy nut?"

"Not sure. He started hanging around here a day or two ago. He seems harmless."

"Bruce, you've got some weird friends."

He shook his head and then said "The killer and the two thugs are not "connected."

I didn't know what he meant and shrugged.

"I talked to an old friend, Tommy Thumbs, at the casino by the track. Tommy didn't know these guys. He told me they're not connected or "made men." Members of the Family don't kill women. Why would they? It's disrespectful and will only get them in trouble. If a woman is unfaithful or

35

steals drugs on her man she might be beaten up, but not killed."

He went on "here's the thing. Tommy said those guys are killers. They wanna kill you. The murder case goes away if you're hit."

Rocky looked at me above his glasses and added "This's for real kid. You're in big fuckin' danger. They could come for you at any time."

He pulled the unlit cigar out of his mouth and looked at it. "There's only one way out of this mess. It's either you or them. And there isn't any time to waste. Here's what I'm thinking. We remove the killer's friends, the two thugs. It'll cost you ten thousand dollars. A buddy of mine has people who will handle it. Don't ask questions about who or how. They'll eliminate the two goons.

"The second option costs more. For twenty thousand dollars, the killer will be eliminated in jail. So you won't have to testify, because there won't be a trial. 'Cause he doesn't exist. Comprendo?" He looked at me above his glasses.

My mouth hung open as I looked at him. "This sounds like a movie. I can't believe what I'm hearing. You're saying that the killer's thugs or the killer himself can be removed, like in killed?"

Rocky looked out the window. "They can be removed. They will no longer be here. They will be gone. Hey, it's either you or them. Kill or be killed."

36

He looked at me to make sure I understood. I'd never seen his eyes so steely cold as he held his stare to see if I understood.

I put my hand over my mouth, trying to wrap my head around what he was saying.

Rocky went on, "The Family isn't into killing these days. It's not good business. They make their money in gaming machines, real estate and loans. But things can still be done. I asked for a favor because I've done a lot of favors in my time. Hey, you don't wanna know any more. Just let me know if you want your problem to go away. How much is your life worth?"

I was speechless. My mouth went dry. I started panting like an old dog. I had trouble catching my breath. I was overwhelmed by the thought that people wanted to kill me.

Rocky could see the troubled look on my face. "Bruce, these are nasty guys. They're killers. You can't talk your way out of it. If I were you I'd pay to get these guys gone."

I felt sick. I was trembling. I felt like my body was going to explode. My mind quit working. All I could do was stare at him.

"Let me tell you a story. Years ago, I'm talking back in the sixties, marijuana was just starting to get big. There was this guy they called "Nose," because he had a long nose that hung down and wiggled when he walked. It was the funniest sight. It looked like a dong. No kidding.

37

"Nose didn't work a nine to five job, but he always had money. He always had a roll of cash in his pocket.

"The cops tailed him constantly trying to figure out how he got his money. He was easy to follow because of his dong. I mean droopy nose. The truth is, Nose got paid cash working for the man. He was a gopher who would do whatever he was told, with no questions asked.

"One day, Nose was told to sell marijuana. He'd never sold drugs before. So he had this big bag of weed in his trunk. The cops knew that Nose was up to somethin' that day. Hell, he had to be doing somethin' illegal. They just had to catch him in the act. The cops saw Nose open and close his trunk a few times so they were curious to find out what was in his trunk. They started tailing him, but got stuck behind a big semitrailer. Nose drove to the track, parked in the front row and carried the sack of pot with him into one of the horse barns.

"It was early so the track wasn't crowded. Groomers were busy taking care of the horses. Nobody paid attention to Nose. Nose found an empty stall and hid the sack in the corner. If anybody saw him walk in they would think that he was carrying a sack of oats or some kinda feed for the horses. Nose walked out whistling while he walked. The stable hands smiled and laughed when they saw his droopy nose wiggle. Nobody had a nose like Nose.

"Well, here's where the story gets good. Fog rolled in like a cloud settling on the race track minutes before the first race. The handlers led the horses into the starting gates one by one. Once all ten horses were ready, the gates opened and the announcer shouted 'And, they're off!'

"The horses were bunched up as they ran around the first turn and disappeared. Disappeared in the fog. It was like the fucking twilight zone. I mean the horses were gone. Out of sight. The announcer was speechless because he couldn't see the horses. They were gone. Lost in the fog.

"Only nine horses ran out of the fog to finish the race. The tenth horse, Red Devil, stopped running when he smelled the pot, jumped over the railing, bucking the jockey off, and ran into the horse barn.

"Red Devil was shot the next day because they thought he was sick with a fuckin' brain disease. The real reason was that he was shot because he ate more than fifty thousand dollars' worth of pot. Do you know what happened to Nose?"

I shook my head. "What happened to Nose?"

"He was never seen again. Someone said that he was bound up and tied to a concrete block and dropped off as alligator bait in the swamp off Highway 90 by Mosca's."

"Good story, but what does that have to do with anything?" I asked. Then I realized that Rocky had effectively distracted me from my worried depression. It worked for a few minutes.

39

Rocky switched back to the topic on hand. "Well, what do you wanna do? Do you want the goons gone or the killer gone? Let's get rid of these guys before they kill you."

Chapter 8

3:00 PM, Friday, July 12th

I sat at Buffa's drinking beer and listening to three women talk about New Orleans music. Apparently they had just taken a music tour of the French Quarter. One of the women looked down at her guide book and read aloud, "In the late eighteen hundreds when much of the country was listening to military marches, New Orleans was dancing to Voodoo rhythms. New Orleans was the only place where slaves were allowed to own drums. Voodoo rituals were openly held and attended by the wealthy and poor. It was in New Orleans where European brass horns blended with the dark rumble of African drums. It was like lightning meeting thunder. Church music was combined with bar music and it became a new music, a happy sound. It was jazz! It made people feel free and alive. People got up and danced. Something magical happened. New Orleans was already a great city where you could dance down the middle of the street during the middle of the day."

The second woman said, "What's really incredible is that music was born here and spread to the rest of the country. Jazz, Dixieland, Rock & Roll, Blues all started here."

The third woman, who had been smiling and nodding her head, while listening to the other women talk, added, "That's why there's so much music here today. It's all over this city, not only in the clubs and restaurants, but on street corners and in the streets, all day long."

The bartender heard the talk and leaned over the bar and said, "That's true. The first rock & roll songs were recorded on North Rampart Street, about five blocks from here." Their heads turned as he pointed out the window.

I looked too to see people walking by. I still hadn't made up my mind whether to go ahead with Rocky's plan to get rid of the goons or the killer. I just wanted the ordeal to end. I didn't like either option. And, I still worried about Carlotta. *Would I ever see her again?*

I remembered that I had stuffed mail in my pocket when I left my house. I pulled it out and set it on the bar. Two envelopes were junk mail, and the third was from the District Attorney's office. I opened it and read that the murder case was being shifted to a different judge and I would be hearing soon when the trial is scheduled. I folded the letter up and stuffed it in my pocket.

What should I do? Should I pay to eliminate the two goons or the killer? My savings account was dwindling fast because I wasn't earning any money. As a professional writer, I couldn't write. Since Carlotta left, my creativity and energy to write was zero. No writing short stories, poems, songs or books, meant no money. Usually I could spit out a short story in a few hours. But not now.

Just then, Rocky walked in the bar with his dog, Booger, and sat down on the stool next to me. Rocky has a loud, raspy voice so I held a finger up to my mouth and told him not to talk about "it" here.

"Hey, no problem, I just took Booger to the park. You remember how she used to sit and watch the squirrels climbing the branches of the live oaks."

"Yeah, I remember. She used to sit still and stare up at the big tree by the fence. The first time we met, you told me she was watching vampires."

We laughed. Times were a lot simpler then.

"Well now she roots out the homeless people that sleep in the bushes. I kid you not. She found a guy this morning and clenched her teeth around his pants cuff and dragged him out. Hell, the guy was all skin and bones. Probably didn't weigh much more than Booger."

I cracked a smile. Rocky always had stories. I guess it was the way he said them that made them funny. "Let's go outside," he suggested.

We stood on the corner and talked about the options. "How quickly will it happen if I go with option one?"

"Immediately. Within forty eight hours for sure."

"Do you mean that within forty eight hours the two thugs will be gone?"

"Yep."

"How'll I know?"

"'Cause you won't see 'em anymore."

"What'll happen to them?"

"You don't wanna know that. Really. Just know that they'll be gone."

Rocky looked across the street at a woman walking a dog. He had a strange look on his face that I had never seen before. He looked like he hadn't shaved in two or three days with his white gray whiskers. His small eyes were dark as he squinted in the bright sun. His black Hogan cap didn't shade his eyes as he finally looked up at me. He added, "Do you want this to end or not? They will kill you for sure before the trial. Hell, it could be any time. You could get run over crossing the street. Or, they'll mug you. Or break into your house. Or a sniper will take you out."

"ENOUGH… ENOUGH!" I screamed.

But he went on, "If you survive to testify you're a dead man after the trial. Although you'll probably be killed before the trial. They'll get you either way. Mark my word. They're not afraid to kill you. And it'll probably happen soon. In fact, I'm surprised they haven't killed you by now. From their view point, the sooner the better to stop you from testifying."

"If you run out of town, the police will catch you and throw your ass in jail and make you testify. And, then you'll be a dead man. Hell, you could be killed in jail.

If you got twenty thousand dollars, there won't be a trial 'cause the killer will be gone."

I shouted, "I DON'T HAVE TWENTY THOUSAND. Besides the goons have seen me. They know what I look like. So, the only option is the first one to have them removed."

I handed him an envelope stuffed with ten thousand dollars. I turned around to see if anyone was watching. Rocky took the envelope and put it into his front pants pocket. Not a word was spoken as we walked away.

Chapter 9

10:00 AM, Tuesday, July16th

"Happy Mardi Gras" a woman wearing nothing, but, paint, shouted out and smiled as she strolled by.

"HAPPY MARDI GRAS!" I said louder as she kept on walking. I hoped she would turn around. It seems that painted women never stop but always continue walking away. This lady was painted purple, gold and green from her face to her feet. It was definitely eye catching. Only in New Orleans, I thought, as I sat on my front stoop people watching.

Wait a minute, I thought, it's not Mardi Gras. It's July. I'm dreaming. Mardi Gras was on March 5th.

It was the first Mardi Gras that I didn't wear a mask or costume. With Carlotta missing I wasn't in a fun mood to party or mingle. I stayed home alone with my door locked and shutters closed. I couldn't quit thinking about Carlotta. *How could she vanish into thin air?*

***

"Hey man, you OK?"

I opened my eyes to see Rocky sitting in my chair. "What're you doing here?"

"Hey. I came over to talk."

"OK. What's up?"

"Ya seen dos boys anymore?"

"No. Haven't seen them nor have I heard anything from the police." It had been two weeks since I gave Rocky the envelope with ten thousand dollars.

"We got a bigger problem now," he said.

I was shocked to hear this. "WHAT? What happened? I thought everything would be OK."

Rocky was silent as he watched four bikini clad girls wearing blue, pink, green and yellow wigs walk by the window.

He leaned over and spoke softly, "It turned out that those guys were members of the Outlaws motorcycle club. They were in town from Chicago. It was kind of a winter vacation thing. When our guy tried to take them out, they resisted. He didn't expect that. They drew and shot him. Before he died, he killed one of them. The other one got away."

My mouth dropped to the ground in disbelief. "What… what… what??? Come on. You gotta be kidding, right? Right?" I searched his face to see if he was kidding.

48

I said, "You're pulling my leg. You're joking? Right?"

"I wish I were," Rocky said looking away. Then he added, "Things are stirred up now. My friends tell me that the biker gang is pissed off. Outlaws are riding in from all over the country. And, the local boys, the Family, are pissed off. There could be fucking World War III happening here any day. Stay low. Don't go out. I mean it. Don't go anywhere."

I didn't say anything. I was stunned. I looked at him. He added, "For some reason the family thinks you're responsible for the mess. There's a contract out for you."

I couldn't speak. I couldn't even breathe. I started gasping and choking for air. It was like a bad dream that was getting worse and worse. I saw a man across the street standing against a lamp post wearing a rubber wolf mask looking at the house. My face felt flush. I felt sick. "I think I'm gonna throw up." I stood up and went into the bathroom.

Rocky was gone when I walked back into the living room. I locked the door and slid over the dead bolt and connected the chain. I could hear people talking outside my window. Oh yeah, that's the way it is here in New Orleans, the Spanish Creole houses are located next to the sidewalks. There are no front yards. Just sidewalks and streets.

49

Correction, make that cracked sidewalks and potholed streets.

I peeked out the window shutters and saw the wolf standing by the lamp post looking at my house. I felt light headed and sat down to think. Bikers and the Mafia want to kill me. The police told me I can't leave town. I'm a sitting duck. My life's over. I rubbed my fingers through my hair. "God, help me. I don't know what to do. "

Chapter 10

8:00 AM, Wednesday, July 17th

I felt a cool breeze and heard a sigh. I opened my eyes to see the old man with the white beard sitting on the sofa across from me. I rubbed my eyes to see if he was for real. He was still there.

"Whoa. How'd you get in here? Who are you?"

He chewed on his lips and said softly "Gregory. Folks just call me Greg."

We stared at each other and finally I asked him, "What are you doing here in my house?"

Again he chewed on his lips as if he were eating them. I could hardly see his lips because of the bushy beard. "I was told that you may need a friend. Well, I'm a friend."

"You sat on my stoop a while back and grabbed my friend when he came to the door."

"Yeah, that was me. I was protecting you."

"I don't get it. Why?"

"I thought he was gonna hurt you."

"But why are you helping me?"

"You were kind to me. Most people don't see me or at least don't acknowledge me. I cleaned the sidewalks and property for your neighbor every day for 14 years. People would walk by and make me feel invisible. They'd never say anything. Not even look at me. But you did. You looked at me. You always had something kind to say to me. It was never anything big, but you introduced yourself and called me by my name. Yes Sir, you'd say 'it's a beautiful day', or 'Good morning, Greg,' or 'How ya doin' today, Greg?' Often it was the only nice words I'd hear all day."

I looked at him. "Greg… you're Greg. You're that Greg? God, I'm sorry. I didn't recognize you because of the beard."

Then I remembered. "But. But. No, no, it can't be you. You died last year. You suffered a heart attack. I went to your funeral. Your wife told me that you died while working at two in the morning doin' cleanup work."

I stared at him. He didn't say anything, but blinked his eyes to acknowledge. He wet his lips and spoke. "You need a friend now. I'm here to help. The word is you're in danger. It's not your time to leave this world yet. Your wife needs you."

"Who told you this?

"Someone you know. Let's just say I know you need help."

Greg was dressed in a neatly pressed white shirt, green work pants and shiny black shoes.

"Remember when you gave me that stick of summer sausage?"

I gave it to him as a thank you gift for his kind words one morning. We had just moved into the house. Our dog was sick the night before and I had to take him outside at two thirty in the morning. I was afraid because the street lights weren't working and I didn't feel safe in the dark.

He was outside washing the sidewalk down with a hose. He waved and smiled and so I walked over and told him that I didn't feel safe. He asked me if I prayed to God. He said if I believe in God, I have nothing to be afraid of because God will protect me. It may sound funny, but his words made me feel good. The next morning I gave him my last stick of venison sausage as a "thank you." I wasn't afraid to go out in the dark after that. *So why didn't I walk with Carlotta that night?*

***

When I came out of the bathroom, Greg was gone. I sat down and read the news on my cell phone. The pitter patter of rain escalated into pounding hammers on the roof and siding. I opened the window for the fresh air. I took deep breaths and listened to the rhythm of the rain because I knew it wouldn't last long. Never does in New Orleans.

***

When it ended, I opened the front door and saw Greg sitting on the stoop. I was amazed that he was completely dry while the sidewalk and street were wet.

"You're back."

"I'm just relaxin'."

"I have to go to Rouses to get some food."

"I'll keep an eye on your house."

I walked away smelling the fresh rain on the street and sidewalks. There were few puddles because the big cracks sucked up the rain like sewer drains. I saw very few people outside until I got to Rouses. Tourists were standing on the sidewalks watching a band.

The band was set up in the street. They were dressed neatly in jeans, long sleeve shirts and hats. An attractive woman wearing a red dress was the band leader. She sat in a chair playing a clarinet with one hand, directing the others, who followed her beautiful melody. She was really good.

She set her clarinet on her lap and said, "Here's a song that you're gonna love. It's called the French Quarter shuffle. It goes something like this.

"Shuffle your feet to the beat…
Down ole Bourbon Street,
Until you hit St. Pete,
Then mosey on over past Decatur,
Until you see Ole Man River.

Stroll along the Moonwalk,
See the people laugh and talk,
Boarding the Natchez and Delta Queen,
Life's fantastic in New Orleans."

I hummed the melody as I walked down the narrow aisles of Rouses and picked out luncheon meat, bread, chips and a twelve pack of beer and placed them on the checkout counter with the security guard standing behind the cashier. I paid and walked away, while the band played on…

Oh yeah stop in the clubs and check out the shops,
See the mules go gitty up,
Keep on movin,' keep on movin,'
Yeah baby now you're groovin'
To the French Quarter shuffle,
The French Quarter shuffle,
The French Quarter shuffle."

***

Greg was sitting on the stoop when I returned. He smiled when he saw me. I raised my hand in greeting and walked past him into the house, unpacked the groceries, sat down with a beer, tore open the bag of chips and started eating them by the handful.

I felt guilty and opened the door to offer chips to Greg, but he wasn't there. I shut the door, locked it, sat down and washed the bag of chips down with beer. I drifted off thinking about Carlotta's disappearance.

She's gone. Gone. But, where is she? I thought about Carlotta every minute after she left. The police finally gave up after a month, but I didn't. I searched and searched until I wore out my shoes. I cried myself to sleep night after night. I lost thirty pounds despite drinking beer. Hell, I didn't feel like cooking. Beer filled me up.

Someone at the NOPD suggested counseling. So I met with a counselor at the Healing Center, but quit after two sessions because I realized I wasn't ready to grieve about somebody who wasn't dead.

Chapter 11

8:30 PM, Monday, July 22nd

I was tired of sitting home alone so I walked over to Buffa's. Singer Anthony Scala, was performing on stage, sitting on a stool, holding the microphone close to his mouth, singing "Sylvie", an old Harry Belafonte song. Anthony had a beautiful voice. He had the ability to make every song his own. He sang music that he wrote and cover songs that he knew the audience enjoyed. I never grew tired of listening to him.

> *"Sylvie, Sylvie I'm hot and dry,*
> *Sylvie, Sylvie can't you hear*
> *Can't you hear me crying?"*

I felt like Anthony was singing to me. "Can't you hear me crying? Can't you hear me crying?" I imagined my wife, Carlotta, saying that. I felt tears on my cheek as I was lost in thought.

The spell was broken when he sang:

"Some Enchanted Evening, You may see a stranger,
  You may see a stranger across a crowded room
  And somehow you know, you know even then,
  That somehow you'll see her again and again."

I felt like I was spiraling down into another world. *"That somehow you'll see her again and again,"* These words made me wonder if I was being sent messages from another world. I squeezed my eyes shut lost in thought until someone touched my arm and said, "Hey Bruce. Are you OK? Did that song get to you or what?"

I opened my eyes and looked at Anthony, sitting on the stool next to me. I nodded. "You're singing was fantastic. The words made me think of Carlotta."

"Hey, I'm sorry man. I feel so bad for you. Has there been anything new?"

"No. Not a thing." I cut my words short. It hurt to talk about her.

I looked at him and smiled. "Thanks for asking. How're you?"

"Busy, busy. I've got gigs five nights a week."

"That's great Anthony. I'm happy for you. Nobody works harder than you."

Candy, the beautiful, ever smiling server, placed a salad and tall glass of ice tea in front of him without speaking. He picked up a fork and started eating. She looked at me, smiled and patted me on the shoulder as she walked away.

I thought it best to let him eat in peace so I didn't say anything about my current troubles as a murder witness. He's a good guy and needed his energy for the next two sets. I put a ten dollar bill on the bar and walked out past two women sitting on a bench by the doorway smoking. I walked around the corner to my house. There was Greg sitting on the stoop.

***

"Hey Greg. How's it going?"

"All's good. No problems."

"That's good."

"Remember God'll protect you."

"Good night, ah… thanks." *Greg made me feel better.*

I grabbed a cold beer out of the fridge and a bag of Chee Wees off the counter and sat down in my chair to think about Anthony's singing *"Can't you hear me crying?"* Was a message?

Then I thought about the words in his song… *"Some enchanted evening… that somehow you'll see her again and again."* It had to be a message. For him to sing these words with so much meaning back to back. Someone was trying to communicate with me.

59

Chapter 12

2:30 AM, Tuesday, July 23rd

POP…POP…POP…POP!

I sat up in bed when I heard gun shots. I passed by Greg who was lying on the sofa snoring with his white beard fluttering in the air. I peeked through the shutters but, didn't see anything, so I unlocked the dead bolt and slowly cracked open the door. I stepped out on the stoop and saw two dark shadows running away on the neutral ground. They had hoodie sweatshirts covering their faces. The second guy's hood fell back as he ran. He stopped, turned to see if anyone saw him, and spotted me. I realized that he couldn't pull his hood up because he was holding a black pistol in his right hand. Our eyes locked for a few seconds, then he turned and ran across Rampart Street into the Treme neighborhood. He looked young.

After they disappeared, I spotted an arm hung over the stoop two houses down from me. I walked over and found my neighbor Leo bleeding. He was moving his mouth trying to say something, but I couldn't understand him. I ran back to get my cell phone and called 911.

Ten minutes later I heard sirens and then flashing blue lights pulled up. Two officers slammed their doors and walked over to check on Leo. I stood on my stoop watching. They were the same police officers that worked the crime scene for the dead woman on Barracks Street. They saw me watching them and gave me a sober *"It's you again"* look.

One of the officers knelt down to check Leo and the other officer asked me what I had seen. I told him that I was in my house and woke up after I heard the shots. Came outside to see what happened and saw two young boys running away and then found Leo lying on his stoop bleeding and called 911.

"He's gonna make it isn't he?"

An ambulance pulled up and Leo was lifted onto a gurney and wheeled away and lifted into the back of the wagon. Neighbors had gathered. Heads were shaking. Women were crying. A man shouted at the police. "THIS IS NUTS. WHY IS THERE SO MUCH CRIME IN THIS CITY? YOU GUYS GOTTA DO SOMETHIN' ABOUT IT."

A woman spoke up. "HE'S RIGHT. WE HEAR SIRENS ALL NIGHT LONG. IT'S GOTTEN SO BAD, I CAN'T SLEEP."

"LOOK AT ALL THOSE GUTTER PUNKS AND DRUGGIES THAT LIVE DOWN THERE ON THE

NEUTRAL GROUND AND BY THE RIVER.
WE'RE AFRAID TO WALK THERE. EVEN
DURING THE DAY."

"SOMETHINGS GOTTA BE DONE."

"THERE'S PEOPLE ON JUST ABOUT EVERY
GODDAMN CORNER BEGGING."

"THIS TOWN IS TOO DAMN LIBERAL."

"YOU POLICE GET PAID TO PROTECT US SO
WE DON'T GET ROBBED OR KILLED. YET THE
ONLY TIMES WE SEE YOU ARE AT PARADES
OR AFTER CRIMES HAPPEN."

The ambulance drove away with Leo. The police
put yellow tape around Leo's stoop. The crowd
broke up and people walked back into their houses
shaking their heads and grumbling.

"Don't leave town" the officer ordered me after
writing down what I told him. He walked away
and then turned around and said, "One more thing.
Do you own a gun?"

"No. No, I don't own a gun."

"Well. That's good. But if I were you I'd
consider getting one for protection now that you're
a witness of two crimes."

His words felt like whips on my back. I felt sick
knowing that Leo might die.

Leo was a good guy. He lived in the old Creole
house for fifty years. It didn't make sense. Why
would anyone shoot Leo? *The shooter saw me.*

J.B. Sensenbrenner

Chapter 13

3:00 PM, Tuesday, July 30th

"That's terrible. I'm sorry to hear about your neighbor. He seemed like a nice guy," Rocky said after listening to me tell him about Leo's murder on the phone. Leo's death was reported on the local news that morning.

"You gotta learn to just stay in your house so you don't get involved in shit."

Rocky was usually a funny guy always cracking jokes and stories. But this time he wasn't laughing.

After a long silence I asked, "Why does bad stuff keep happening?"

"So you heard gun shots, looked outside, saw kids running away leaving your neighbor bleeding to death on his front stoop. One of the kids saw you watching him run away. Is that right?"

"Yeah."

After a few seconds, Rocky said "Hey, I gotta work now. I'll get back to you."

I set the phone down and thought to myself that I can't live here anymore. This town's too much for me to handle. I thought about how tripping on the cracked sidewalks used to be my only worry. Then my wife goes out for a walk and never returns. And now I'm a key witness in two murder cases and a target to be killed. I pictured an army of bikers, Mafia, and kids that want me dead. Talk about depressing.

***

I must have dozed off because I woke when I felt a cold draft on my neck. I rubbed my neck and blinked several times.

"Don't worry. Everything will turn out fine."

Greg was sitting across from me. When he saw me look up, he said again "Don't worry. Everything'll turn out fine."

"HOW CAN YOU SAY THAT?" I screamed.

"'Cause I know. And it's the truth. Trust me."

"BUT, HOW DO YOU KNOW THAT I'LL BE OK?"

I lowered my voice and went on. "There are people… a lot of people that want to kill me. I'm a witness. They want me dead."

Greg stared at me and waited to see if I was finished. I wasn't and said "How can you say it'll be OK? My wife's missing and probably dead because of me. Now, a lot of people want me dead. I feel like I can't go outside. The police told me not to leave the city. I feel like a prisoner on death row.

God, I miss my wife so much." I broke down sobbing.

After a few seconds Greg said, "I just know. I know you'll be OK. Trust me. Everything'll turn out OK." He glared at me, but, in a warm, knowing way. He reached out to pat my arm.

He's crazy I thought to myself. He's crazy. "YOU DON'T KNOW."

"But I do know. You've been a good guy your whole life. You've been kind and good to people. We all make mistakes. We have to learn from our mistakes and move onward. Life's a journey."

I took a deep breath and said, "Greg, I don't go to church. I've been praying to God for help, but, I don't think he hears me. I don't know how I can go on. My wife left me. The Mafia, biker gangs, and kids want to kill me. I can't fight them all. I can't win. I'm doomed."

Greg stared at me and said, "Don't give up. God loves you."

***

5:00 PM

Rocky was sitting at the bar waiting for me. Booger was sitting on the stool next to him with her paws on the bar.

"How ya doin'?" he said.

I sat down and looked down the bar at the other people. There were eight people in the bar. What I

67

liked best about Cosimo's was that it was a "neighborhood bar" with mostly local people.

I turned back to face Rocky and said, "Terrible."

He looked at me and said, "You're in a helluva tough spot."

"Do you think?" I sarcastically responded. I thought about telling him about Greg. Dead Greg. Or, Greg the ghost, telling me that everything will be alright. But, I knew he wouldn't understand, so I skipped it.

"I'm surprised you left your house to walk here. Hell, it's dangerous for me to sit next to you." He squirmed in his seat and looked around.

"I'm trying hard to hang on. The truth is that I've never felt so low in my life. I don't know how much longer I can hang on."

Rocky took the stubby cigar out of his mouth and said, "Well, I told my friends that you were gone. Out of town."

A voice behind me said, "Tell him to tell his friends that you're back in town. That you want to meet with them."

I turned around to see who said that, but no one was there. *Maybe I'm hearing things.*

I looked at Rocky. "Tell your friends that I'm back in town and wanna meet with them."

"Are you nuts? They wanna kill you. You got one of them killed. Now, all hell could break loose with the biker gang at war with my friends. Shits gonna hit the fan any time now and you're right in the middle of it with fucking bullseyes on your back and forehead."

"Please set up the meeting," I insisted and walked out.

***

I had no appetite when I arrived home. Didn't even want a beer. I felt frustrated and desperate. I plopped down in my chair, closed my eyes and tried to think about something positive to replace the negative circling in my mind.

I thought about the trip that Carlotta and I took ten years before to Tanzania. It was a great adventure that I'd never forget.

It was early January when Carlotta, son Tom and I were riding in a Land rover in the Serengeti. Our driver/guide Larry had filled up the Land Rover with petro at the Ranger station at six thirty in the morning. We were now bouncing up and down on a dirt road in search of the "migration," which consisted of thousands of zebras, wildebeests and Thompson gazelles.

We were amazed at seeing so many ostriches and giraffes running away from us as we drove through the acacia trees. We had no idea that there were so many of them. Our driver, Larry, slowed, as we watched elephants walk along the edge of a scrubby woods, pulling branches down to eat the leaves. We were speechless from seeing so many animals as we drove more than thirty miles away from camp in search of the animal migration.

Larry whose native tongue was Swahili said in broken English that he'll take a short cut to find the migration. He turned on a dirt trail, which had no tire marks. We hadn't seen another human being since the petro fill up at the ranger station.

I was excited, riding in the front passenger seat next to Larry. I encouraged him to drive faster before the scorching sun and rising temperatures would force the animals to hide and seek shade. Larry drove the Land Rover like a highly skilled jockey at Churchill Downs as he bounced up and down clenching the steering wheel with both hands. He turned off on a faint trail winding west along several kopjes (rocky outcroppings) and stopped as we approached a pond covering the trail. The pond was caused by the heavy rain the night before not draining through the high rock table. Without saying a word, Larry turned off the engine and got out to check the water depth. He shook his head when he got back in.

"Is it very deep?" I asked him.

"Doesn't look too deep."

"Yeah, it's from the rain last night. You can drive through it. Drive fast and don't stop. This Land Rover has four wheel drive and will go through anything like a Sherman tank," I said, encouraging him.

He stepped on the accelerator and pulled the stick shift into second gear. The Land Rover raced ahead, splashing water above the windows until stopping after twenty feet. There was complete silence. The water was *deeper than we thought. We weren't quite half way through the pond. When Larry stepped on the pedal, the wheels spun, spitting water and mud in every direction. Instead of moving, it sunk.*

He shifted gears from forward into reverse and stepped on the accelerator. The wheels spun but didn't move. Instead we sunk deeper. Larry continued trying, shifting back and forth. We were sinking deeper into the water. The wheels spun kicking out wet mud in every direction.

We saw wildebeests, zebras and gazelles grazing a couple hundred feet across the water. It was the migration. We almost made it.

Monkeys were playing on the big rocks in front of us on the left. There were bushes on our right. Prior to our trip I had contacted the Center for Disease Control in Atlanta to learn about health issues to be aware of in Tanzania. I carefully read the eleven pages of warnings and remembered specifically a warning to avoid contact with fresh water from ponds or streams because of harmful bacteria skin infection.

Larry told us to stay inside. He jumped out into the water, circling the Land Rover, bending down to look at the wheels, scratching his chin and muttering mostly in Swahili, but, we understood him to say "Not good. Not good. Stuck. We're stuck."

Unfortunately, there was no way to call for help. There was no radio, no cell phones, no walkie-talkies, no GPS. Nothing. We were more than thirty miles from our camp. It was too dangerous to walk back without

71

weapons. Despite the water hazard warnings, Tom and I decided to jump out into the knee deep water. We talked to Larry and made a plan that we would push from the front bumper while he tried to shift from forward to reverse so it would back out. Mud and water splattered on our faces, shirts and legs. No matter how hard we tried, we couldn't budge the heavy Land Rover. My words haunted me now when I called it a Sherman tank because it was heavy like one. We couldn't budge it. I remembered gripping the bumper and feeling its sharp bottom edge cut my fingers while I tried to lift and push. We tried and tried and finally gave up. We were stuck too deep in the clay muck.

We felt the warmth of the rising sun as we searched for rocks and stones to fill in the ruts. We planned to fill up all four wheel ruts, so the wheels would have traction to back out.

The search for rocks and stones proved tougher than we thought because Larry ordered us to stay within ten meters of the vehicle because of the threat of a wild animal attack. It took us more than an hour to fill up the left wheel rut. In fact there were so few rocks, that we started breaking sticks off of the bushes. When we finally got the right wheel rut filled, we noticed that the left wheel rut was empty. Larry had removed the rocks.

"Hey, Larry. Did you takes the rocks out of the left tire rut?"

He was sweating profusely and said "Yes. I removed the stones because they are plugging it up and blocking the tire."

72

We looked at each other and couldn't believe our ears. Tom patiently explained to him that the plan was to fill up the ruts with rocks so we could drive over them. The rocks would provide traction for the tires. We wanted him to understand but didn't want to make him feel bad, because Larry was our guide and we didn't want him to lose confidence. It seemed that he was on the brink of a nervous breakdown. We needed him to help us find our way back to camp. There was no way we could find our way back without him.

The sun was right above us. It was scorching hot. Our sweat mixed well with the mud and water on our faces, shirts and legs. We had been stuck for more than six hours. Suddenly, Larry started running down the trail. He was waving and yelling. We looked beyond him and saw nothing but heat waves. We realized Larry was hallucinating. I ran after him and grabbed him around the waist. We couldn't afford to lose our driver and guide. I told him on the walk back that we would be OK.

At one o'clock, Tom, tapped me on the shoulder and whispered that he don't want Mom to hear, but, look over there at the big round rock. I gasped when I spotted a honey colored female lion slowly dangling her tail, watching us. I calculated that she was about a hundred yards away, about the size of a football field.

As we continued to work on the ruts, I looked over at the kopje and hour later and saw two female lions sitting on the same round rock. Zebras, wildebeests and gazelles across the pond were running and barking, enticing the lions. We were stuck in the middle.

73

Although we continued filling in the ruts, we started working on a new idea to drain the water away by digging small canals away from the wheels.

By four o'clock the water level was noticeably lower, so we tried to push it out again, but couldn't budge it. I looked over at the round rock and saw four female lions lying together watching us and the animals across the pond. Tom and I both watched them constantly now as the shadows were growing larger. I worried when they would climb down to start their hunt for dinner. And, would they target us or the barking zebras or wildebeests?

We didn't give up. We worked until dark trying to back out while the lions watched us. Carlotta noticed us looking at the rocks and saw the lions. She jumped in the Land Rover, slamming the door and started crying. WE ARE DOOMED. WE'RE NEVER GONNA GET OUT OF HERE! WE'RE GONNA DIE! WE'RE GONNA DIE!

At six o'clock, light was fading fast. Larry told us to get into the Land Rover. He handed each of us small paper bags, which was our uneaten lunch. I opened mine up and found a boiled egg, a banana, a hard roll and a warm bottle of soda.

We were tired, dirty and hungry. No one spoke as we ate. When we finished, we tried to get comfortable for the night. Carlotta lied down with her head on my lap and continued crying. "WE'RE GONNA DIE! WE'RE GONNA DIE! I DON'T WANNA DIE!"

By seven o'clock it was pitch dark. It was so dark that the windows looked like they were painted black. I have never experienced a darker time. We couldn't see anything outside.

After eating a hard roll, I opened the window only a couple inches for fresh air and thought about going outside to pee. I put my ear to the window and heard the loud, rumbling, guttural roar of a male lion coming from the round rock area. It was a scary powerful, haunting sound. I decided that I didn't have to pee after all and quickly shut the window. The lion sounded hungry and all powerful. I'm sure his airy roar could be heard for miles.

I wasn't able to sleep. I was aware of the risk of malaria coming from mosquito bites but, I was even more afraid of being killed by a lion, so I opened the window sparingly, only an inch or so, almost hourly, during the night for fresh air and to check on the location of the lions. Whenever it was opened I heard the loud, rumbling, breathy roar of the male lion from the same position on the rocks, until four o'clock. There was no lion roar. I listened intently. There was silence.

I fumbled around in my back pack and pulled out a small flashlight and stuck it out the window, scanning the field. Whoa! It shinned on a golden body, then another and another. Oh my God! Lions were circling us. Maybe Carlotta was right, we were gonna die. I could feel her trembling and sobbing as I held her. I pulled the flashlight back and shut the window as tight as possible. I checked to make sure the door was locked. I

75

looked around and saw that everyone was sleeping,
including Carlotta. No one else saw the lions moving in.

***

I woke up in a cold sweat when I heard sirens screaming by the house. Somehow I felt better hearing sirens instead of roaring lions.

Chapter 14

10:00 AM, Thursday, August 1st

Rocky picked me up in his cab. "You sure you wanna do this? Personally, I think you're crazy. You don't know what you're getting yourself into."

Greg sat in the back seat. I turned around to look at him. He nodded and said "It'll be OK. Don't worry. God'll protect you."

Rocky drove down Esplanade and turned left a block before Broad Street. I didn't catch the street name because the street sign was missing. He pulled up to a large sheet metal building and got out. I followed him to the door. He turned and said "Wait here."

Greg and I waited on the crumbled concrete driveway. There must be something about the concrete in New Orleans as it's either crumbled or cracked. I heard loud talking going on, as the door opened up. Rocky yelled "GET IN HERE!"

I walked in and saw a big, heavy set man with a cigar in his mouth wearing a leather shoulder holster with a black handgun sticking out sitting behind an old gray military desk. There were several dark haired men sitting in wood chairs against the wall. One guy stood by the door.

Rocky said "This is Bruce Paul."

I stuck out my hand, but, the big man didn't reach for it. He simply stared at me like I was a piece of shit. I felt like it.

"Sit down."

I sat down rubbing my hands on my pants legs.

"Tell the man what happened. Tell him the whole story."

I told him that "I was walking down Barracks Street about ten in the morning, minding my own business, looking down at the cracked sidewalks, which were terrible in that area, when I heard screams and shouts across the street. A man burst out, leaving the door open. He ran around the corner out of sight. I walked over to look inside the house and discovered a woman's body lying on the living room floor. I checked for her pulse and didn't find one. I called 911 and reported the murder. The police came. After telling my story twice. I was told to stay in town. A short time later I was sitting on a bench near Jackson Square and saw the killer talking to two other men. I called 911 to report him. Two police cars came and arrested them.

"The next day I identified the man in a police lineup. But, on my walk to the police station I was beat up and left for dead."

I looked over at Rocky. "I paid money to have the killer's buddies that beat me up removed. I understand that the hit got botched and two people were killed, but, one of the killer's friends got away. This is all I know. Swear to God on my mother's grave."

I looked at the big man who remained expressionless. His dark eyes were burning a hole through me. Rocky broke the silence and said, "Bruce's a standup guy, Sam. He's my friend. He's a good guy who got himself in a jam. That's why he wanted to tell you his story. Now, can you help him?"

The big man moved the cigar to the other side of his mouth and said "Yeah. But, it'll cost."

I stared at the man. Rocky shifted his feet and said "he gave me ten thousand. I gave it to your boys."

"Yeah, but, now I need twenty thousand to pay for the funeral and take care his wife."

They both looked at me. I nodded and muttered "Sure," even though I didn't really mean it. The big guy turned around in his chair. Rocky motioned for me to leave by pointing at the door. I slumped down in the chair and didn't move as I thought about what he said. I wondered where I could get twenty thousand because there wasn't that much left in my savings account. Rocky nudged me to leave. I got up and walked out.

We drove back to my house without talking. Finally, when he parked in front, Rocky said, "Let me know when you got the twenty grand."

Chapter 15

10:30 PM, that night

I wasn't tired because I was thinking about the meeting with "the man" and couldn't decide what to do.

"You did the right thing, meeting with him." Greg spoke from where he was sitting on the sofa. I looked up at him.

"Do you really think so?"

"Yeah. You did the right thing. You brought it to him. That earned his respect. Now he'll help you."

"I hope so."

The phone rang. "Hello."

"I'm outside your door. Let me in."

I opened the door for Rocky. He sat in my chair before I could. "Can I get you a beer?"

"Yeah."

After taking a long sip out of the bottle of Abita Amber, Rocky said, "Here's the deal. The man said for twenty thousand he'll remove the contract that's out on you locally and the hit from those

Chicago Outlaws. No one'll be out to get you. But the deal is, you can't testify in court."

He added "If you testify against the guy, all bets are off and you're a dead man, either before or after the trial."

I started trembling. I was shaking so much that I couldn't think straight. Greg put a hand on my shoulder and said, "Tell him there's no deal. The man's a killer. You'll testify."

Rocky watched me like a bird watching a worm wiggle in and out of the grass.

"I can't agree to that deal. Tell Sam I appreciate his offer. But there's no deal. I'm gonna testify."

"You're signing your own death warrant. You don't wanna do that."

"Listen. I already identified the guy in a police lineup."

"Don't matter. If you're dead, you won't testify in court when it counts. They'll make sure of that."

Greg tapped me on the shoulder again. "Don't worry. You'll be OK."

I turned towards Rocky and said, "Tell Sam there's no deal. I'm not paying twenty thousand."

Rocky stood up shaking his head and said, "I can't tell him that. I can't tell him that. He'll kill you with his own hands." He walked out the door chewing on his cigar and mumbling in Sicilian.

***

I fell asleep on the sofa. Sometime later, sirens screamed by with blue flashing lights turning my living room into a seventies disco. I woke up with a stiff neck. I felt a cold draft.

Greg was sitting in my chair watching me. I rubbed my neck, stood up, stretched and peeked out the window. Police cars sped away. I saw someone sitting on my stoop. I opened the door to tell him to move on.

"It's me Benny."

It was my old college roommate, Benny Tailman. I rubbed my eyes and looked at him again. He had gray hair and mustache, neatly combed, a light blue polo shirt and white shorts. It was him alright. He was a sight for sore eyes. I cleared my throat and asked him to come inside. *The odd thing is that he died from a liver problem eight years ago.*

We continued our friendship after college by getting together once a year to deer hunt in northern Wisconsin. He owned a collection of rifles that he inherited from his father. His favorite was an old Winchester 30-30 carbine. He swore that it was the best gun for shooting deer in the brush.

God, it was good to see him. We had been best friends and had so much fun together. There were so many good memories. One year, on Wisconsin's opening day of deer hunting, we walked out of the cabin at five o'clock in the morning. It was black dark and freezing cold. We whispered "Good luck"

83

to each other and separated, walking down different trails into the woods. He walked up a big hill, sat against a tree and waited for daylight. I walked further into the woods about a quarter mile away. It started snowing an hour later which seemed to lighten up the woods before sunrise.

BANG!! A shot rang out 30 minutes after daylight. I knew it had to be him because he was the only hunter on the big hill. A few minutes later I heard three whistles which was the signal that a buck was shot. I walked over to find Benny bending over a nice six pointer. It was only seven o'clock. I congratulated him with a big hug. He told me to go back to my stand and hunt. I told him that it's early, so I would help him drag the deer back to the cabin. I knew he would've done the same for me.

He was a sight for sore eyes.

"I heard you need help."

I looked at him. It sounded like him. It really was Benny. My mouth hung open. I rubbed my eyes again, wondering if I was dreaming. I stuttered, "Yeah, yeah, I've got problems."

"That's why I'm here. I wanna help. You were always there for me when I needed help. You even helped me with homework and tests. Remember the time I grabbed your blue book off your desk during the Psychology final exam? Ha, ha. Hell, my best times of my life were spent with you. Now, I wanna return the favor and help you."

Greg reached out and said, "Hi, I'm Greg." Benny grabbed his hand and shook it, "Nice to meet ya. I'm Benny."

Chapter 16

8:00 AM, Friday, August 2nd

I walked to Cabrini Park with Spike. After I was about thirty feet inside the gate I heard someone shouting "Everybody, everybody, good morning! Everybody, everybody good day!" I turned around in time to watch a grey haired man riding a bike. I smiled and waved at him as he faded away. It was the third time I had heard the ole man sing as he rode by on his bike. This time the words really hit me. I couldn't get them out of my head because they were catchy. When I returned home, I sat down and wrote a song. It goes like this.

"There's an old man who rode a bike down our street,
Singing a little song with a sweet melody and a
simple beat,
Everybody, everybody good morning, everybody,
everybody good day!
This silly little song is all I have to say,
Singing everybody, everybody good morning,
Everybody, everybody good day,

Kindness and joy to you, have a very good day!
I wondered about this angel of music as he faded from
view,
It made me smile to hear his words, this much I
knew…
Singing everybody, everybody good morning,
Everybody, everybody good day!
This silly little song is all I have to say,
Singing everybody, everybody good morning,
Everybody, everybody good day.
Kindness and joy to you have a very good day!
I heard his bike got stolen, but then came that
familiar voice down the street,
He was smiling as I watched him walking in his bare
feet, singing…
Everybody, everybody good morning,
Everybody, everybody good day!
This silly little song is all I have to say.
I bought a shiny new red bike
To give him as he walked by
But, he never came again my way,
I heard that he died later that day.
I walked out to the grave yard and found his stone,
And laid the bike gently down
And as I walked away, I swear I heard him sing…
Everybody, everybody good morning,
Everybody, everybody good day,
Kindness and joy to you as you go on your way
Have a very good day!"

***

I sang the words to myself over and over. It felt good. It was the first good piece of writing that I had done since Carlotta walked out. I was jarred out of my writing dream world when I heard a different song…

"I see trees of green, red roses too,
I see them bloom for me and you,
And I think to myself what a wonderful world."

It was my cell phone. "Hello."

It was Rocky. "I'm in front of your house. Let me in."

Funny. I didn't have a ring tone with Louie Armstrong singing "What a Wonderful World." How did that get on my phone? I thought I was losing my mind.

I opened the door and let Rocky in. Of course, he sat in my chair before I could. He held his cigar up as if it were a weapon to ward me off. I sat on the sofa between Greg and Benny. Rocky cackled when he talked. Sometimes his voice rattled in the mornings like an old lawn mower. "Umph. Errrrg. Umph. Here's the deal."

We looked at him and waited for him to clear his throat. "I talked to the man. I told him that you said 'no deal.' That you're gonna testify in court."

I was dying to hear what he was going to say next. "And? What did he say?

The man said, "He doesn't approve of guys killing women. He says the guy deserves to be punished. He's OK with you testifying and will cancel the contract and make sure the bikers call off their hit."

I couldn't believe what I was hearing. Benny and Greg smiled and patted me on the shoulders and said, "We told you it would be OK. It's OK now."

"Does he mean he'll call off the hit by all parties, Chicago and New Orleans?"

"Yeah. There'll be no hit. At least not by them. You still gotta worry about those kids that killed your neighbor."

Greg smiled and Benny grinned at me. I felt both their arms patting me on the back. It felt a little weird, but under the circumstances, it felt good.

Rocky continued, "I gotta be honest with you. Bruce, you're a straight shooter. I know that and told Sam that. You just got yourself in a tight spot. A real tough spot. I gotta a confession to make. I only paid five thousand of the ten thousand that you gave me for the hit. Hey, they took it. OK? So, I gave Sam the left over five thousand. I told him that's all you got. He's OK with that. Maybe if I would've paid more for the hit on the two thugs, it wouldn't have gotten botched up. I take the fall for that."

Rocky looked dejected. "I'm sorry for that. Hey, the cab business is tough. Uber is killing me. Hey, but it turned out good. So I gave Sam the rest of your money."

He got up and walked out before I could speak.

When he left, Benny spoke first, "You did the right thing. You're OK now."

Greg added "I told you that it'd be OK."

"Yeah, but I still have a problem. I'm a key witness for Leo's murder, too. And those kids know where I live and what I look like."

Chapter 17

9:00 AM, Saturday, August 3rd

I drove to the Downtown Fitness Center on St. Claude Avenue and parked in the lot by the food Co-op. I walked up the long stairway and entered the work out room. "Good morning Lenny."

"G' mornin'. How ya doin' today?"

"Doing better. Today's better than yesterday." After sliding my membership card through the check in, I walked by several circuit training machines and stopped to greet a good friend, David, who was kicking his leg back and forth on a lift raising machine.

"David. How ya doin?"

"Hey. Good man. Good to see you back in here working out. Since your wife's been missing I hadn't seen you work out much.

"So you're good."

"Yeah, you're right. You're right. You're right."

I sat down in front of an arm strengthening machine and pulled the two hand pulls, but, couldn't budge them. "David, did you set the weights at 200 pounds?"

I stood up as he walked over to sit down and pull the hand pulls. He did it one time and said, "I've got other things to do today."

I walked back to the room with the elliptical machines and put a white sweat band over my forehead, plugged in ear buds, and turned on the TV. I changed the channel to *Law and Order* and hit the Quick Start button. Working out relieved a lot of stress but it didn't take my mind off getting killed or Carlotta. After twenty minutes the sweat started pouring out of me.

I looked in the mirror to see a young man with orange tipped dreadlocks start up the tread mill machine. I hadn't seen him work out before. He fumbled with the control buttons, so I knew he wasn't a regular. The treadmill started moving. Although I was watching the small TV screen on my machine, I sensed that the guy was looking at me. I slowly turned to look at him and said "How ya doin?"

He didn't answer but looked away. After working out for sixty minutes I stepped off the machine, still feeling the guy's searing stare, I walked into the restroom and bolted the door. I took my time, washing my hands and splashing cold water on my face, hoping the guy would be gone when I walked out.

He was waiting in the hall way. I stopped when I recognized him. He looked like Leo's killer.

Just then, the door from the ladies rest room opened and a muscular woman walked past me, making the guy move out of her way. I followed close behind her with the guy following.

Lenny wasn't at the front desk, which was unusual, so I continued walking outside with the guy following me. I saw Dan, a uniformed security guard talking to Cap Black, a "safety advocate" and Dwayne, the maintenance manager. "Hey guys. How ya'll doin'?" I walked up to them, making it awkward for my stalker.

Cap spoke first. "We're doin' OK. How's your workout?"

"I've got a problem. This guy seems to be following me." I motioned with my hand in front of me and pointed a finger behind me to the guy standing by the door. All four of us turned around to look at the guy. He wasn't smiling. His face was still shiny from the treadmill work out.

Cap was the kind of guy who was never intimidated. He was 6-3" and 245 pounds of solid muscle. He walked straight at the guy and when he was inches away said, "What do you want?"

The guy didn't speak. Cap towered over him and said louder, "Are you going to buy food or do something? What's up man?"

As I said, Cap was a big guy, who looked like an ex-New Orleans Saints tackle. The guy tried to walk around, but, Cap stuck his arm out blocking his way. The guy swung at Cap and missed. Annoyed from missing his first attempt, he swung again, but this time his fist bounced off Cap's chest. Cap grabbed the guy's shoulders, pushed him to the ground, and stood over him with one foot pinning the guy down. Cap towered over him, watching him like a giant super power. The guy shook his head and hissed. Cap pulled him up on his feet, held his arms, while Dan handcuffed him.

"This is the guy that killed my neighbor."

They looked at me. "Are you sure?"

"Yeah, I'm sure."

Cap called his contact at the police station. A car pulled up in the parking lot ten minutes later, and two officers got out. Cap and Dan walked the kid to them. They pushed him down into the back seat and shut the door. Cap told them what happened. I told them that I recognized him as my neighbor's killer.

Cap walked with me to my car and said, "He won't bother you again. If he does, call me."

Chapter 18

9:00 AM, Monday, August 5th

I woke up early feeling good because Leo's killer was arrested. One less person to worry about. I heard a rooster crowing outside the bedroom window. It reminded me of Key West or Samoa, where chickens patrolled the neighborhoods eating insects. They're part of the island culture. People love the chickens. They don't eat them. Heck, they don't eat beef either. They eat fish.

I drove to the fitness center, worked out on the elliptical and circuit training machines, drove home, showered and sat down, alone, wondering where Greg and Benny were. I swear I only took two breaths before the phone rang.

"Hello."

"Bruce, this is Detective Broussard, I need you to come down to the station. We caught two young teenagers in your neighborhood last night in a botched robbery attempt. We want you to look at them in a line up to see if either one is the killer of your neighbor Leo Stone."

I explained to him that I was involved in the killer's arrest at the healing center. He was aware of that but still insisted that I come down to identify him in a line up.

"Yes. I can come. When do you need me?"

"Ten o'clock."

"I'll be there."

I felt a cool draft. When I put the phone down, Greg was sitting across from me.

"How'd you do that? I didn't see you come in. How do you just appear?"

Greg looked at me and smiled a big toothy grin. "That's just the way it works now. I can go where I want and be where I wanna be by just thinkin' about it. I felt a vibe that you may need my help and poof! Here I am."

"Well you must've heard me on the phone. I have to go down to the police station to identify the kid who killed Leo."

"Yep."

"I still don't understand why he was killed."

"Leo was a good man. He was always outside washing his car or painting the trim on his house. I knew him for 14 years. We used to talk trash about the Saints 'til they won the Super Bowl. Leo loved to drink Bud Light."

"Greg, what happened? Why would anybody wanna kill him? Leo was harmless. He wouldn't hurt a flea."

"He was an easy mark. Sitting on his stoop like a pigeon day after day, night after night. The kids tried to get in his house. A woman friend told them there was valuable stuff there. It was a botched robbery. Leo wouldn't let them in. He stood up to them and told them to get lost. That's when one of the kids pulled a gun. Leo didn't back down. He fought the kid and the gun went off.

"The kid you saw shot him. That's when you ran to the door and looked out and saw him running away."

"How did you know all that? Where were you?"

"I was around. I saw it."

I went to the bathroom, shaved, and showered. When I came out Greg was gone. At least I couldn't see him. I got dressed, brushed my hair, and put on my shoes. I grabbed an apple out of the fridge, locked the door, and walked over the cracked sidewalks to the police station. I wondered about the sidewalks. Why were they so bad? I mean some of the cracks were so bad you could lose a dog in them. I stumbled as I thought about them. Head down, watch where you're walking. I was breaking a sweat when I arrived at the station. I reported to the officer at the reception desk that I was there to see Detective Broussard.

***

Detective Broussard walked out extending his hand. "Thank you for coming down on short notice." He explained that they caught the kids in a robbery on Bourbon Street at one thirty in the morning. They tried to rob two middle aged men. The men resisted and clobbered the kids. They were charged with attempted armed robbery. Usually kids do multiple crimes until they get caught.

"We think these kids were friends of the kid who tried to attack you yesterday. You were lucky Cap Black was there."

He led me down the hallway into the same line up room that I had sat in weeks before. This time five young males were led into the room. Again, thank God, there was a one way mirror hiding me from them. I immediately recognized the third kid because of his orange tipped dreadlocks and missing front tooth. I waited until each one was told to step up and then told Broussard,

"It's number three. It's number three."

"Can you identify the other ones?"

"No. His partner had a hood on and ran ahead of him. But, I saw number three because he turned around and his hood fell back. I recognize him. He was holding a gun."

"Ok. Thank you Sir. If there's a hearing we will notify you when it is scheduled. Meanwhile, please stay in town."

I walked out into the lobby area and saw Rank talking to a uniformed officer. He saw me and broke away.

"Well, well. If it isn't the lone witness. How ya doing?"

"Better. I just identified a killer for another murder."

"For which murder?"

"For my neighbor, Leo Stone."

"Yeah. Broussard told me that you saw the kids running away."

"Stay safe."

"Thanks."

Chapter 19

11:00 AM

After I was done I strolled through the card readers, artists, and brass bands by Jackson Square and went into Muriel's. It was one of my favorite places to eat because it was never over run with tourists, even though it was in the center of the French Quarter. It was too early for happy hour, but, not too early for lunch. I ordered a shrimp po-boy and an Abita Amber.

I felt a cool draft and rubbed my neck. Although the bar was empty when I walked in, Benny was sitting on the corner bar stool. He saw me, grinned, picked up his drink, a scotch and water, and moved over to the stool next to me.

"How's it going Stretch?"

"It's going. Geez, you're the first one to call me Stretch since our Marquette days. No, I take that back. You called me that whenever we got together until… you… ah… died."

I looked at him realizing what I said. I looked over at the bartender to see if she could see him.

"Are you holding up OK?"

"Yeah. Things are better."

We looked at each other and I asked him, "Am I the only one who can see you? Wait, Greg sees you, too. Can the bartender see you?"

"No."

"How can you drink?"

"I like drinking. Hey, don't worry about me. You're the one who needs help."

We were interrupted when three women walked in and sat down on my left. I smiled at them and then turned towards Benny and said, "It's not easy. Ever since Carlotta left, my life's been a roller coaster, up and down, slow and fast. I'm just trying to hang on, or I'll go crazy. It's been seven months. I don't know where she is. Or what happened. I was blindsided. She went for a walk and never came back."

He looked at me and said calmly, "I saw her. She misses you."

I was blown away. "What? Where is she? Where'd you see her?"

"I don't know where she is. But I saw her. She misses you."

"She was crazy about this place. She loved New Orleans. She loved living here. We didn't argue. I don't have a clue why she…." Suddenly, a chill came over me and I froze. My mind went blank. I blinked several times. Benny was gone. The stool to my right was empty. And there was no glass of Scotch on the bar.

The server set a white linen napkin in front of me with sterling silverware and a crystal goblet filled with ice water. She looked at me with her dark brown eyes. "Are you feeling OK? You were talking to yourself."

I didn't know what to say. I couldn't tell her the truth that I was talking to a dead friend. "I just feel kinda down today. Really down."

She didn't push it as she moved over to wash glasses behind the bar. I looked up at the TV in the corner showing a soccer game from South America. I looked back at the bartender and asked, "Have you ever lost someone you love?"

I must have surprised her as she moved closer and asked me to repeat it.

"Have you ever lost someone you love?"

Her big brown eyes seemed bigger as she looked into my eyes. "No. I haven't. That's so sad."

Since the women had left with their drinks in "Go cups," there was no one else in the bar to overhear, so I told the bartender my story.

"My wife loved the city, the music, the food, the people and all of it together. She could never get her fill of it. She left one night. I thought she went to Frenchman Street to check out the music. She had gone there hundreds of times by herself. This time she forgot her cell phone. Left it on the kitchen counter. I found it after she left, when I tried to call her when she didn't return. She never came back. I never saw her again." I broke down sobbing.

"Oh, my God, how awful. I feel so bad for you. When did this happen?"

"It happened on January 7th, the day after her birthday. I walked the route she always took down Esplanade to Royal, past the R-Bar, to Frenchman. I looked for her and asked in every club if they had seen her on both sides of Frenchman Street. I walked back and forth. I didn't sleep that night. I called the police. Nothing. No one saw her. Some of them remembered seeing her several days before, but, not that night. I posted pictures of her missing on windows and telephone posts."

"Did the police find anything?"

"Nothing. After a few weeks, it seemed that they wrote if off that she left on her own. There was no foul play. They told me to notify them when she comes home."

The server reached across the bar and put her hands on top of mine. "I'm so sorry." She had tears in her eyes as she rubbed my hands.

Chapter 20

8:00 PM, Wednesday, August 6th

I was sitting at a small table with friends Dana and Matt at Cock a Doodle, a small club, and popular local place for live jazz, rock, and funk music.

We were eating wings and ribs watching Dean Chase, New Orleans great troubadour, setting up his equipment on stage. He was one of our favorite entertainers. He had been touring in Ireland and California, so it was the first chance we had to see him in several months.

After introducing himself to the audience, he recognized us and nodded. Then he led off by singing…

> *"Shadows in the night,*
> *I see shadows in the night,*
> *They're such a scary sight,*
> *Seeing shadows in the night.*
> *I watch them in my chair,*
> *See 'em moving here and there…."*

Dana and Matt were super people who were always fun to be with. Carlotta had always loved their company. We went out to different restaurants and clubs with them and would often trade books or give each other extra chocolate cupcakes, bars or cookies. As a single man, they continued their friendship with me. I valued their friendship more than they would ever know. It helped me hang on.

They quit asking me if I had heard any news about Carlotta. After she left, they helped me search for her by walking the streets and posting pictures of her.

"We cancelled the trip to Europe," Matt said.

"Oh, I hope you didn't do it because of me."

Carlotta and I had planned to go with them to France in September.

Matt looked at me carefully, to make sure he didn't offend me, and said, "No. No. We just thought we would postpone it for now."

Chapter 21

8:30 PM, Thursday

Buffa's Bar owner sat down next to me at the bar. He leaned over, and asked if I heard anything about Carlotta. I shook my head "no."

"I'm so sorry. Please let me know if there is anything we can do to help."

"Thanks."

After a few minutes he turned to me and said one of their outside video cameras showed the two guys fighting and shooting Leo on his stoop."

"Can you see their faces?"

"Yeah. Yeah you can see their faces clearly. It's incredible how sharp the picture is."

"That's good. Did you give it to the police?"

"Yeah. They picked it up this morning."

"Great."

"They'll be off the streets for a long time."

"That's great news. I remember when you installed the cameras a few years ago. It's good to see that they work so well."

"We invested quite a bit of money."

"I've been meaning to ask you this question for years. Why'd you name your place "Buffa's?"

"I didn't. It was called Buffa's before I bought it. I did some research on the name and learned it might be a Sicilian nickname for a huckster or joker."

I felt a cool draft when I saw Benny sitting on a bar stool by the window. He held up his glass of scotch, smiled and toasted me. I nodded. The bartender gave me a funny look. I turned around to look at the stage.

Anthony Scala sat on a stool holding a mike nodded to his pianist and started singing…

> *"If I were sitting in Heaven,*
> *You'd feel the warmth from my eyes,*
> *And re-a-lize,*
> *That I'm watching you,*
> *Yes it's true, that I see you,*
> *While Angels sing…."*

Chapter 22

8:30 AM, Tuesday, August 12th

There were no roosters crowing this morning. They were replaced by crows cawing in the neighbor's trees. Hurricane Katrina had greatly reduced the bird population in New Orleans. There weren't many birds. That's why the brassy caws of the crows didn't bother me.

I walked to Cabrini Park with Spike, my black lab, who was 15 and still with it. I saw Rocky's cab parked on Dauphine Street. He was sitting on the concrete curb inside the park watching his bob-tailed dog Booger rolling on the grass with Stubby, a two year old Corgi.

"Hey, what's happening mon?"

"I identified Leo's killer in a police lineup last week. The killer and his friend were arrested for a robbery attempt. Since they fit the description of Leo's killer, I was called in to identify them. Buffa's gave the police a digital video from their street cameras showing the two kids shooting him when he refused to let them in his house."

111

"That's good. Sometimes things turn out OK. Glad they caught them so quick. There're way too many robberies around here."

"And killings," I added.

I looked away at a big brown dog that entered the park off leash with his owner trailing behind. Spike didn't bother to lift his head. Rocky asked, "Did you know that New Orleans is a big ghost town? They claim that New Orleans and London have the most ghosts in the world."

"That's interesting. Wonder why?"

"Hey, I heard there's a woman who has special powers. She's supposed to be the 'real deal.' She works in front of the Cathedral. Her name is Madam Sherry. I've had cab customers talk about her when I drive them to the airport. They say she's amazing. Some said that she really sees things. She sees ghosts."

"Do you think she could help me find Carlotta?"

He took the stubby cigar out of his mouth, looked at it as if he was considering eating it, and said "What the hell. It's worth a try. If I were you I'd talk to her."

"What'd you say her name is?"

"Madam Sherry."

***

I walked Spike back to the house. When I walked in I was hit by a cool draft (and immediately knew) that Greg was sitting on the sofa. He looked at us, reached over, and rubbed Spike on the head. Spike didn't react to his touch, but growled. Greg removed his hand. "He can't feel me pet him, but he knows I'm here. He's a smart old dog."

I called Detective Beamer. As an NOPD detective, he was overworked with too many cases and not enough hours. He led the search for Carlotta for weeks after she disappeared. He and his team searched our apartment for clues, talked to neighbors, club owners and friends, and ran me through the wringer, which I tried hard to forget. But he came up with nothing. Nothing. He told me that they've seen it happen before where couples break up, married or unmarried, and one of them leaves without warning. He felt bad for me but was convinced that Carlotta left me. Period. Finally, he had to move on to work on other cases.

I left all her clothes, shoes, purses, earrings and jewelry where she left them. I had never given up finding her. Cap Black was the one who convinced me to let go. He said, "It's time to let go. You did everything you could to find her and so did the police. It's been six months. Just let go. Life goes on."

So, I stopped looking for her, but didn't give up hope. The murder on Barracks Street and then the murder of my neighbor Leo interrupted my endless mind circling search for Carlotta. I can't say it was good thing, 'cause I was almost killed but I survived, and can focus on Carlotta again.

Part of me was numb or dead. I had been married to Carlotta for 30 years. We were a good team. We had a lot in common. We both loved New Orleans and its great food, incredible music, interesting people, endless parades and festivals. In short, New Orleans was the most fun city in the world. We were happy.

The last time I saw her was when I was sitting at the table writing a song about ghosts on my lap top computer. It was titled "Shadows in the Night." It was storming out and made me think of ghosts. When the storm passed, she wanted to go for a walk. I didn't. We argued, and she left.

She never came back. I never saw her again. It sounds like a broken record, but I never saw her again. I slowly erupted like a volcano walking the same route on Esplanade to Royal to Frenchman, back and forth, back and forth. Talking to every human being that I saw, asking them if they had seen Carlotta, I was exhausted. I didn't sleep that night. I hoped she would come back.

In the morning, I called the police. I called every friend on the phone to see if they had seen her, or if she had stopped at their place. I went ballistic.

When Detective Beamer showed up, I was frantic. I blurted out and jumbled my words in panic, that there must be something wrong.

Something seriously wrong. Because she always came home. But this time she didn't.

I remember lying in bed that night unable to sleep. I thought about the lions circling us in the Serengeti, and how I held her tight and promised her that we would survive. I got up and drove the car back and forth on every street, like a matrix, looking for her. I felt terrible. I felt so bad that somehow I had failed her. I was in a black hole and didn't know how to get out of it.

Chapter 23

12:00 PM

My phone buzzed. "Hello."

"Bruce, this is Detective Rank. I have some bad news. Murder suspect, Ralph Mastroni, broke away from the police van this morning. He escaped. We have an all-points bulletin alerting all law enforcement to look for him. He was being transported from a holding cell at the station to a higher security unit. I wanted you to know. Please lock your door and stay safe. I'll call you immediately when we catch him. Don't worry. We'll catch him."

I put the phone down on the table and thought to myself that my life had become a paperback novel. How could anybody make this shit up? I was a key witness for two murders. The killer for the first murder escaped. The suspects for Leo's murder were in jail. My wife's missing. And I am under orders to stay in town. Now I have to stay in my house. And I'm seeing ghosts. I walked to the

117

refrigerator, grabbed a beer and took a long swig, wishing it was something stronger.

Chapter 24

11:00 AM, Wednesday, August 13th

I sat in my chair thinking about the killer on the loose. Would he try to kill me in my house? Greg must've read my mind, as I felt a cold draft and opened my eyes to see him sitting across from me.

"Hey Bruce. Remember what I told you, not to be afraid? Well, don't be afraid."

I looked at him and somehow felt better. Then I remembered Rocky telling me about a medium named Madam Sherry and that she often works by Jackson Square in front of the Cathedral. "Greg, I gotta leave. Gotta find Carlotta."

I walked down Chartres Street to the square and saw swarms of tourists, artists, musicians and several card readers and mediums. I walked slowly, stopping in front of each card reader and medium hoping to spot a sign or name tag. Seeing none, I asked a lady "Are you Madam Sherry?"

"No baby, but I can help you. Please sit down."

"I need to talk to Madam Sherry."

119

A woman sitting at the next table overheard and told me that she knew Madam Sherry. She explained that she was her niece. She said that Madam Sherry would be back in a half hour. I thanked her, and told her I would return. I walked over to the Lucky Dog vendor on the corner and bought a foot long hot dog and a bottle of water. I sat down on a wrought iron bench where I could eat and watch for Madam Sherry. The Lucky Dog was delicious and made me wonder why I didn't eat them more often.

While I was eating, I watched a lady dressed in white with her face and arms painted white, holding a white umbrella above her head, stand perfectly still like a statue. She stood on the top step by the corner of the cathedral. She'd curtsey whenever people dropped money in the white bucket in front of her. Jackson Square has no shortage of talent.

A brass band started playing "When the Saints Go Marching In." Tourists loved it. All in all, it was entertaining just to sit and watch the real life circus going on with so many different characters.

A woman walked by wearing a red scarf wrapped around her head, much like the legendary Creole voodoo Queen Marie Laveau. In fact, it kind of gave me the chills to look at her because of the close resemblance.

I wiped mustard off my lips and tossed the napkin into the trash container next to me. I took a

120

few deep breaths and walked over to her. She waved her hand for me to sit down in the empty chair. Her niece leaned over and whispered to her that I had been waiting for her. She looked at me with the darkest eyes I'd ever seen and said, "I'm Madam Sherry. How can I help you?"

I felt that I was already under her influence. I was lost in her deep dark eyes and had trouble speaking.

"What can I do for you?"

I felt very uncomfortable. I was intimidated. I didn't know where to start. She saw my hesitation and suggested in a softer voice, "It'll work best if you start at the beginning."

After taking a deep breath, I told her "Last January my wife left me. Well, she didn't really leave me. She went for a walk on a Monday night to go down to Frenchman Street. At least that's where I think she went. She'd done this many times before. She liked to hear the live music. This time she never came back. I searched and searched for her. The police searched and searched. We never found her. No one has seen her. She vanished. She's considered a missing person."

Without speaking, she reached out and held my right hand. I thought she would read my palm. Instead she held it in both her hands and closed her eyes. Her hands felt warm. It was several minutes before she opened her eyes. I'd never seen a look

121

like that on anyone's face before. She had seen something. Then she stared deep into my eyes.

I tried to ask her what she saw, but I had no voice. No volume. I cleared my throat so I could speak up "Erg...erg...What... what did you see? What is it?"

She said very clearly, "I saw your wife. She was sitting on the steps of a small house, crying. Her eyes were red. She said she wants to go home. But she doesn't know the way."

My mouth dropped open. I looked into her eyes wanting to know more.

"Do you call her Bunny?"

"Erg... erg... ah yes. I call her Bunny because of her endless energy."

She continued staring at me without blinking or talking. So I asked, "How do you know that? I was the only one who called her Bunny."

"She told me to tell you that so you know it's her."

I was blown away. I took a deep breath and said, "Where is she? Do you know where she is? Please, please tell me, so I can find her and bring her home."

Madam Sherry closed her eyes as she said in a low, bass voice, "She's here. She's not far away. I... I... I can't see her anymore."

Her head hung down almost touching the table, as if she was dead from the exhaustion of the vision. Her niece grabbed her shoulders from behind and said, "Please leave her alone. Please go, now. Go!"

Madam Sherry looked limp. She was lifeless. I walked away with answers and more questions. *But I now had hope. Benny was right, she's alive.*

Chapter 25

10:30 PM

I was so excited about Madam Sherry's vision that I couldn't sleep, so I started reading "ATLAS SHRUGGED." It was a big eleven hundred page hardcover book that felt like it weighed 20 pounds. It was a very dry and sobering read. I thought it would distract me from reality or at least tire me out from holding it.

It did neither as I couldn't quit thinking about Carlotta. I was too excited learning that she was alive and wanted to come home! Benny had told me she was alive, but somehow hearing Madam Sherry tell me and knowing her nickname, Bunny, made it real. My mind kept circling around the thought that she's alive and not far away, as I fell asleep.

***

I woke up in the middle of the night thinking about Madam Sherry. *"She's here. Not far away."*

I had never told Madam Sherry that I called her Bunny. It was an inside joke between us. I would often kid her about having so much energy like the energizer bunny because she wanted to go out all the time to see music. Madam Sherry had no way of knowing that I called her Bunny. She must've really connected with her. No one knows that I called her Bunny except for me. *She must've really seen her. But, where is she? If she's here, where is here? How can I find her?*

Chapter 26

10:00 AM, Thursday, August 14th

As soon as I was done with my breakfast of yogurt with granola, I walked down to Jackson Square to look for Madam Sherry. This time I walked fast literally pounding the pavement. I didn't care about the cracked sidewalks. I flew over them. It was early, the artists and tourists were there, but there was no Madam Sherry. There was an empty spot where her table had been the day before.

I sat down on a bench next to the railing to wait. I read a paperback book written by a New Orleans author about an actor who returned to the city to discover how his father died. After a couple hours, I was disappointed that she didn't show up, so I walked back home.

Greg, with his white beard, was sitting on the stoop. It seemed like he had taken on the permanent role of being my personal body guard. He sat with his arms folded across his chest.

"Hey Bruce. How's it going?"

"Not good. She wasn't there."

He followed me in. I grabbed a beer from the fridge and offered him one, but he turned it down. I took a long sip and then asked him if he believed in ghosts.

He looked at me to see if I was serious. "I certainly do. There are a lot of ghosts in this town."

"So I heard. So I heard."

"Why do you ask me that question?"

I looked at him. "Well, you're a ghost. Right?"

"I don't think about it that way. I'm a being. I'm to help you."

I told him about yesterday's meeting with Madam Sherry. "Somehow I need to break through into the spiritual world. I think Carlotta is trapped and can't get home. Madam Sherry told me that she's here. She's close. I've got to find her to bring home."

Greg looked at me, considering what I said. "Everything'll work out. You'll find her. It'll be good."

I didn't really know what he meant. If what he said was profound or just kind words, so I pushed him. "What do you mean? How do you know?"

He looked at me with his eyes opened wide, not blinking. His eyes seemed warm and comforting as if he was speaking to me without saying words. I began nodding my head as I accepted what he was communicating. Somehow I understood that what he was saying was true, that everything will be OK. I felt better.

When I reached for my beer, Greg was gone. Then it dawned on me that I had just asked a ghost if he believed in ghosts. Had I offended him by using the word "ghost?" The word "spirit" seemed to be more politically correct. If Carlotta was here, she would have corrected me to use the proper word.

Chapter 27

11:00 AM, Saturday, August 16th

It was three days since I'd seen Madam Sherry. I checked each morning and asked other mediums, but no one knew where she was or when she'd be back. If they knew where she lived, they wouldn't tell me.

I stood in the empty spot where she'd been, looking at the other card readers and mediums, thinking maybe her niece was nearby, but didn't see her, so I walked down Decatur Street to clear my head. I chuckled at the long lines of tourists standing in front of Café Du Monde waiting for their famous beignets and coffee. I stopped to pet a brown and white spotted mule drinking water from an old concrete trough, waiting for tourists to climb aboard his buggy. The mule seemed content with his job of giving tourists buggy rides around the French Quarter. I looked into his eyes and wondered what he was thinking. I rubbed his nose and left.

I walked through the gate into Jackson Square and went straight ahead to the stunning statue of Andrew Jackson riding his horse as if it were during the Battle of New Orleans in 1815. People were busy snapping pictures of each other standing in front of the statue. I walked around a large water fountain and then out the gate in front of the Cathedral.

I looked left and was surprised to see Madam Sherry wearing the same red scarf wrapped around her head busy talking to someone. I waited patiently looking at a painting of a man with rabbit ears taking a stroll in the clouds. I wondered what it meant. Finally, the lady left.

I walked over to her table. "Madam Sherry, where've you been? I've been looking for you, but you weren't here."

"Please, sit down."

I tried to act cool putting my hands on my legs and sitting up straight. "I have more questions."

She looked at me and said calmly, "I spoke to your wife. Her real name is Carlotta, not Bunny."

"Yes. Her name is Carlotta. What else did she say?"

She never blinked. Her deep dark eyes stared deeply into mine. "She was crying. She misses you and says she's sorry that she left."

"Where is she?" I blurted out.

"She seems to be trapped. As though she's caught in a spider web in an evil place in a different time."

I stared at her not quite understanding what she was saying. Her eyes were closed now as she continued speaking.

"She can't find her way home. She wants to come home. She wants to see you. But she can't."

"Where is she? Do you know where she is? Please tell me." I pleaded with her.

She didn't speak. Instead she reached down for her brightly colored hand bag which was heavily embroidered with African dancers and set it on the table. She pulled out a pen and small note pad and scribbled…

192 Old Valley Road
11:00 PM, Sunday

She looked at me and blurted, "Take this. Come to this place. She may be there."

133

Chapter 28

11:00 PM, Sunday, August 17th

I leaned forward in the car on the steering wheel to see the road because of the heavy rain pelting the windshield. I stopped several times to lower the window to read the numbers on mail boxes. I pulled up to a place that was poorly lit except for a gas light. There were several cars parked and buggies with mules tied to a steel fence. I parked and walked up to the large three story, wood frame, plantation style house with a wrought iron balcony. A live oak tree, with its branches spreading low with Spanish moss dangling in the wind, seemed to be guarding the old house from intruders. I ducked under a branch and was slapped in the face by wet strands of Spanish moss. I felt a vibration like droning bees swarming around their nest as I approached the house.

Large steel numbers, "1 9 2", were displayed above the door. I couldn't find a door bell, so I knocked. No one came, so I knocked harder and harder. I was about to pound both fists on the door when it opened a crack. I said, "I am here to see Madam Sherry," as loud as I could. A person wearing a brown hooded toga opened the door wider, just enough for me to squeeze in sideways. Once I was inside, the door creaked shut and a big wooden brace was put back in place.

The vibration and humming grew louder as I was led through a hallway lit by flickering gas lanterns to a courtyard overflowing with people. My guide never spoke but blended in with the crowd who were all wearing the same brown hooded robes.

The lighting was dim as gas torches flickered around the courtyard. I moved slowly through the crowd looking at each hooded face for Carlotta or Madam Sherry. There was an electricity in the air, an energy that I'd never known before. Suddenly the drums stopped. The silence was eerie. The crowd moved to the courtyard walls creating an empty space in the middle. A drum started beating slowly as a person walked to the center, stood, and turned slowly around to look at the silent crowd standing in a circle. All eyes were on her when she flung off the robe. She was totally naked. I gasped. It was Madam Sherry.

More drums. I couldn't see them, but it sounded like several more drums joined the solo drummer. Madam Sherry danced slowly at first with her hands waving above her head as she moved around the circle of people. As the drums beat faster, she danced faster and faster, until she was spinning around the room. She kicked her legs high and threw her arms in the air until I thought she would fly away. Perspiration made her face and breasts shine in the flickering light. I had never experienced anything like it. I was mesmerized.

I started feeling light headed. The sounds, smells, and drink were all foreign to me. My mouth was parched, so I drank from a clay goblet that was put in my hand. It tasted sweet like coconut and rum. I drank too fast as it ran down my face. Someone filled it up, and I swear it was never empty the rest of the night.

Two more people tossed off their robes and joined dancing with the shining woman who looked upward until all I could see were the whites of her eyes. They were men, thin and muscular, with taunt muscles. They danced around the woman as bees would fly around their queen. Their hands reached for her every body part, but never touched her. Their bodies bumped, rubbed, and slid down each other, as though they were one not three.

A hand pulled me up although I didn't remember sitting. I blinked and wiped my eyes as someone loosened my belt and my robe fell off. Everyone's robes fell to the floor. We were all naked. But it was OK. It felt natural, so natural. I danced. Everyone was dancing to the hypnotic drumming. I danced like I had never done before, synchronized by the beat with the other men and women. I could feel sweat covering my body with a sheen, and it felt good. I felt light. So light, as though it was my spirit dancing and not my earthly body. I felt weightless as I blended into the swirling mix circling the room.

Without warning the drumming stopped. Everyone stepped back. Madam Sherry stood in the middle. I noticed that she had a white fleur de lis tattoo on her shoulder. She held up a dark red rooster by its neck with its wings flapping wildly. In her other hand, she held a machete, its blade shining from the flickering light. She raised the cock up and swung. Poof! Its body dropped to the ground, with its wings flapping wildly. She released her grip on the big knife and let it drop to the stone floor and raised the cock's head with both hands. Its blood dripped on her face and into her mouth. She seemed in ecstasy as its blood ran down her lips onto her breasts and stomach.

The drums started pounding louder as she closed her eyes and strolled around the room with her blood soaked, glistening body. I couldn't take my eyes off her, as she danced. It was the most tantalizing sight I had ever seen. She threw her head back and flailed both arms wildly in the air. As the tempo picked up, her legs seemed to be another pair of arms as they kicked equally as high. Ribbons of blood streamed down her face and breasts and mixed with her sweat adding a luster that made her glow. She looked supernatural.

Chapter 29

11:00 AM, Monday, August 18th

A loud, annoying buzzing woke me up. I swatted at it several times as if it was a big house fly. Feeling the hard plastic of my cell phone brought me to my senses. I didn't know where I was. I was naked, covered by a sheet. I felt cold. Cold all over. My feet were ice cold. It took a while to wake up. It was an odd feeling as though I had come back from a trip from outer space.

What time is it? And, why am I naked? I looked at my cell phone. It was eleven AM. There was a missed call from Rocky.

I looked around the room but didn't see my clothes. The phone buzzed again.

"Hello."

"Hey Bruce, it's me, Rocky. I'm worried about you. I called you three times this morning and you didn't answer. That's not like you. Are you OK?"

"Yeah, I'm OK. Just tired. Had a long night. Come on over. I'll tell you about it."

141

"I'm parked in front of your house now. Let me in."

I looked around the house for my clothes, but, couldn't find them. I grabbed fresh underwear, red shorts, and a Jazz Fest shirt out of the dresser, put them on, and walked to the door.

"Come on in."

"You worry me, man." Rocky said as he sat down in my chair.

"I'm OK. Just had a long night. Why is it so cold?" I said rubbing myself with both hands.

"I was worried that something happened to you. Thought that thug got you."

"No. I'm OK."

"So what'd you do last night?"

I took a deep breath. "I went to a strange party. Remember, you told me about that Medium down by Jackson Square, Madam Sherry?"

"Yeah. Did you see her?"

"Yeah. I met her a couple times now. She's good. You were right. She's connected to the spirit world. She found Carlotta. Well, I don't mean found her. But she connected with her. She told me that Carlotta wants to come home."

"Really. Really? That's great. So, where's she?"

Madam Sherry said "She wants to come home, but can't."

"What does that mean?"

"Exactly. That's what I asked her. She told me that Carlotta wants to come home but can't. She said Carlotta's sad. She saw her crying. She gave me a note to meet her at 11:00 Sunday night at an old plantation house on Valley Road. She said that Carlotta may be there. I went to the house and was led into a courtyard where there were people wearing hooded robes. Drums. The only music was from the beating of drums. Madam Sherry danced. Whoa, did she dance. I never saw anything like it before."

Rocky looked at me funny. "It sounds like some kind a voodoo service. They're very secretive about actual gatherings. Very few people know about them. They're invitation only."

"It was really strange. It's hard to explain, but it seemed supernatural. I'd never experienced anything like it before. "

Rocky tilted his head looking at me. "So did you see your wife?"

"I looked but didn't see her. People wore hoods. Once the dancing started, I didn't look for her any more. I couldn't. It was so crowded. I drank a coconut flavored potion and got lost in the drumming and dancing after that. I felt good. It was hypnotic. I must have passed out. In fact, I don't remember coming home. I woke up when you called."

Then I remembered, "My clothes are missing."

We both looked around the living room and didn't see anything. I rubbed my shoulders, "Why do I feel so cold."

Chapter 30

3:00 PM

Just as I was about to walk down to Jackson Square to look for Madam Sherry, someone threw a brick through my window. I stormed out to see a young kid in a too long T-shirt running away towards Rampart Street. "HEY. WHAT THE HELL YOU DOIN'? STOP. STOP."

I knew it was useless to chase after him. He never looked back as he disappeared down Esplanade. I walked back into the house and felt a cool draft on my neck. Greg was sitting on the sofa.

He watched me kneel down to pick up the broken glass. There was a note tied to the half brick. I pried the string off and unfolded the paper. I read it aloud…

"Don't look for me.
I can't come back.
Let me be."
C

145

I sat down and read the note again and then handed it to Greg. Before he read it he said, "Dat kid didn't mean to hurt you. Is this your wife's handwriting?"

"Yeah. What do you think it means?"

Wish we could catch him to find out who gave it to him."

Greg said, "I'll find 'im!" and vanished.

Ten minutes later he came back dragging the kid by the shoulder into the house. "Tell him. Tell him who gave dat note to you."

The kid looked at me and then back at Greg, "Who gave dat note to you?"

The kid spoke softly, "A woman told me where you lived. She asked me to get the note to you. I never saw her before. I didn't mean to break your window, I swear."

"What'd she look like?"

"She had dark hair. She was shorter than me. She was nice. I mean polite. But, but…"

"But, what?" I asked.

"She seemed sad. Real sad."

The kid turned to Greg and said, "That's all I know. Can I go now?"

"First you help clean up the mess you made."

After picking up the pieces of glass, the kid apologized and left.

Greg had been a bouncer at a club on Bourbon Street for years until he roughed up a guy too much. The story goes that two guys started fighting over a young woman. One guy claimed that she was his property. The other guy said people don't own other people. That's slavery. Pushing turned into shoving and hitting. Greg stepped in to break up the fight and threw both guys out of the bar. The guy who claimed to own the woman came back in the bar with a gun. Greg went ballistic, knocking the gun out of the guy's hand and accidentally breaking his neck. Greg was arrested when the police came. Thank God there were plenty of witnesses who stood up for Greg and told the police that Greg was the bouncer and "the good guy" in the fight.

I read the note again.

> *"Don't look for me.*
> *I can't come back.*
> *Let me be."*
> C

Once again, I had more questions than answers. I wasn't sure what it meant. But knowing she's alive and now communicated with me bolstered my hope.

Why didn't she want me to look for her? Why can't she come back?

Chapter 31

8:00 PM,

I sat at the back bar at Buffa's waiting to hear a young singer perform. He was accompanied by a pianist who I didn't recognize.

> *"Cara Mia, why must we say good bye?*
> *Each time we part my heart wants to die.*
> *Darling hear my prayer*
> *Cara Mia fair*
> *I'll be your love till the end of time...."*

I loved this song. I was amazed at the singer's beautiful voice. I had requested this song for several years but was turned down by other New Orleans performers, probably because it took a special voice to reach all the high notes. Then I thought about Carlotta. Was it somehow connected to Carlotta? Was there a message that I should not give up searching for her? That *she will be my love until the end of time?*

149

Benny was sitting on the bar stool by the window. "Hey Stretch, that's your favorite song isn't it?"

I didn't see him when I came in. I was startled to hear his voice. "Yeah, yeah I really love that song. There's so much emotion in it."

"He sang it almost as good as Jay Smith. Remember Jay and the Americans?"

"That guy's got an incredible voice. Hey, Benny, you said that you had seen Carlotta. Right? Where had you seen her?"

He looked at me and then at the stage. "I saw her standing on that island or median." He pointed outside towards the river.

"When?"

"It was quite a while ago. Before I saw you. Maybe early January."

Several people walked in and sat down at the bar. When I turned around to ask Benny more questions, he was gone. I had never heard the door close. I walked home thinking about where Benny saw her. The "neutral ground" by the river was the site where many train hoppers and gutter punks, as they are called by locals, hung out. *What was she doing there?*

Chapter 32

8:00 AM, Tuesday, August 19th

I was sitting at Café Du Monde waiting to meet an old friend from Wisconsin who had emailed me a few weeks before that he was coming down to New Orleans and wanted to get together.

I waved and stood up when I saw him walk in.

"Hey Barry. It's good to see you?"

"Hi Bruce. Good to see you, too."

"How's your drive?"

"Good. It's an easy drive. We stopped over in Memphis. Saw Graceland. Ate BBQ. We got here at midnight. It's funny I did all the driving but Carla is wiped. She's sleeping in."

"How's Carla's knee?"

"Good. She can walk better than ever. I have trouble keeping up with her."

"I know how that goes."

The server, wearing a white paper Café Du Monde cap and apron, stood at our table. We quickly gave her our order for beignets and coffees, while a trumpet player played outside the railing, slowly walking up to tables hoping for tips. It seemed that you could never escape hearing music in this city. It's everywhere.

"How are you doing? Are you holding up OK? It's gotta be rough."

"I'm OK. There are good days and bad days."

"How long has she been missing?"

"About eight months now."

"Let me get this straight. Her body was never found right?"

"Right. Never found. The police consider her a missing person."

I shook my head and wished the conversation wouldn't have turned so quickly onto Carlotta. What else can be said? It was a conversation killer. I didn't want to tell him about Madam Sherry or the party. "Hey, do you guys want to visit a plantation? I heard there's a new one. I mean an old one that's being updated on River Road that's supposed to be realistic with people acting like plantation owners, workers and slaves."

"Yeah. That sounds good. Let's do it tomorrow. Is it OK if Carla comes?"

"Of course. I'll pick you up at 10:00 AM."

Chapter 33

10:30 AM, Wednesday, August 20th

It was overcast and raining as we drove slowly on a dirt road, splashing through puddles, finally reaching the front of an old plantation house. Strangely, we were the only car there, with the exception of an old gray pickup truck. Spanish moss dangled from the long reaching branches from the centuries old live oaks in front of the house. Large white Roman columns stood like colossal soldiers guarding the house. The front porch was wide and wrapped around the corner of the house. It was lined with wood chairs and a table in the corner. As we walked up the brick pathway to the house, a young girl dressed in a one piece burlap sack dress ran up to meet us.

"Good morning ya'll!"

We were surprised to see her. Or I should say, it seemed that the girl was surprised to see us. "Hi, we came to tour the plantation."

"Oh no. There are no tours here."

"What do you mean? We heard that it was open?

"No Sir. It's not open for other people yet."

"As long as we're here, can we look around?"

"No Sir. You better go." She turned around when she heard front door open. A tall man with long black hair and mustache stepped out and shouted, "WE'RE NOT OPEN FOR THE PUBLIC."

He walked down the porch steps passing an old black sugar kettle filled with rain water. It looked like it could be used today for washing.

"I'm Jacque Landry. I own this property."

"Hi, we came out for a tour. She told us that you're not open for tours yet. Can we walk around as long as we're here?"

"Apparently you people don't listen. We don't do tours. Sorry you wasted your time driving out here."

He turned around to walk in the house, but stopped and faced us and pointed to his left. "As long as you're out here, ya'll visit Oak Alley, the Whitney or Laura plantations. They're all open for tours." He turned to walk back into the house.

He had a deep burning look in his eyes. It was creepy as though he were from another era. Another time. None of us spoke as we walked back to the car. After we got in the car Barry said, "There's something strange about that guy and this place."

Carla added, "I had the feeling there were people looking at us through the cracks and shutters of those shacks. I saw people that were dressed alike. It looked like they were wearing shirts and pants made out of brown burlap bags. They watched us. There's something wrong. Something's not right."

Barry said, "There was a large garden. Looked like vegetables growing in it. The house and shacks looked like they were two hundred years ago. It was like stepping back in time. I wonder when it will open up to the public."

"Maybe never. It's privately owned. They don't have to give tours. There wasn't a gift shop or ticket office anywhere."

"You're right?"

"It could be operated as a farm or a large working plantation. It looked like a cotton field way back and a long sugar cane field next to it. The big wooden building behind the house is probably used for processing the sugar cane. The workers must live in those small houses in the back."

"What bothered me was that Landry had a pistol and a whip on his belt. Why?"

"It takes a lot of labor to make a plantation run. Cheap labor."

We drove down River Road about a mile and slowed down when we saw live oaks lining both sides of the walkway to a large plantation house. It was a magnificent sight and helped wash our negative thoughts about the "working plantation."

"This is Oak Alley," I said. *But, there was something odd that stuck in my head about the working plantation.*

Chapter 34

7:30 PM

It's good to have friends. It's always great to have friends visit from out of state. Maybe it's because you look at things differently when people visit New Orleans for the first time. I felt good. Maybe the best I've felt since she left. We parked in the back lot and walked into Cock a Doodle Doo's. Dan, the owner, reached out to shake hands. I introduced Carla and Barry. He laughed and said "I was reaching for your money. The cover charge is $10 each tonight. Dean Chase's performing."

I laughed, but felt a little embarrassed. I dug out $30 and gave it to him. We walked towards the bar to order drinks. Dean was sitting at the bar sipping a cold beer talking to an attractive young woman. "Hey Dean, how ya doin'?"

Dean wore a Sinatra type hat and blue open neck shirt showing his necklace of bones. "Hey man. Thanks for coming out."

I introduced Carla and Barry, then ordered two Canebrake drafts and a glass of Chardonnay from the pretty, petite, blonde bartender. She was already filling the chilled glasses with beer before I finished giving the order.

We found a round table with three stools in front of the stage and sat down. We ate BBQ wings and potato salad, while Dean was busy connecting speakers and microphones on the stage. Dan was scurrying around setting up more chairs and tables. He walked by and said "Dean's popular. He always draws a good crowd."

Dean stood up to the mike, looked over the crowd, smiled big, and shouted, "WELCOME TO COCK A DOODLE'S. I'M DEAN CHASE. I'M HAPPY TO BE HERE AND HAPPY YOU'RE HERE."

Dean told stories about his recent tour. "Hey, it's fun to travel and see the sights and especially the people. But, what I love best is coming back to New Orleans. This is the most fun place on this planet," He started strumming the guitar and sang...

> *"I am a humble troubadour singing you a song,*
> *It's a song of love that won't be long,*
> *Let me tell you what I know,*
> *It may not be much, but here I go...."*

Everyone was laughing at the lyrics and joined in by singing the chorus.

"Love is the most wonderful thing,
That makes bells ring,
And make faces smile,
And bodies embrace for a while,
Love is the most wonderful thing,
Love is."

Dean had the audience in the palm of his hand for the rest of the night. It was a great performance. I thanked and hugged Dean after the two plus hour show. It was like hugging a Saint.

160

Chapter 35

11:30 AM, Saturday, August 23rd

Carla and Barry left early to drive back to Wisconsin. They planned to stop along the way at Natchez and then at a prehistoric Indian settlement in western Illinois. It was a good visit. I enjoyed their company and cherished their longtime friendship. Their visit took my mind off my worries and search for Carlotta.

***

I was biting into a shrimp po-boy at Parkway Bakery with Rocky slurping down a roast beef po-boy with gravy and meat spilling out all over the table.

"I told you the roast beef po-boys are messy."

"Yeah, but, they're good. Damn good." He said while chewing and squeezing it with both hands.

I looked at him and laughed. Just the way Rocky said things was funny. He wiped his mouth but missed the corners. There was a pile of napkins in front of him. "You know when I was younger, I loved sex. Who didn't, right? That's what life was about. But, now as I get older, I love food more. Food has replaced sex. The problem is that I like it so much that I can't get into my own pants anymore."

I laughed and so did the couple at the table behind us. Rocky was a hit. He fed off the success of his joke and added. "You know my dog Booger, right? Well, Booger had a stroke. Or at least I thought she had a stroke, 'cause she couldn't jump up on the bed to go to sleep. So I lifted her up onto the bed. She started gasping, coughing and badly wheezing. I thought she was dying, right? So I gave her mouth to mouth by covering up the two little holes in her nose with my fingers and then blew air down her throat."

"Ha, ha. Did that work? Hell, it must have, she's still alive."

"Yeah, I figure, I saved her life. But, she almost bit my nose off." He pointed to red teeth marks on his nose. He put the po-boy down and started laughing at himself.

After lunch, Rocky dropped me off. Greg was sitting on the stoop.

When I unlocked the door and sat in my chair, Greg was already sitting across from me on the sofa.

"How's lunch?"

I was surprised that he knew. Then I calmed down realizing as a ghost he knows more. "I just ate a delicious Parkway shrimp po-boy. Sorry, no leftovers."

"No problem. Got some news for you."

"Good or bad?"

"Good. You know dat boy who threw that brick through your window?

"Yeah. What about him?"

"He won't be coming around here anymore."

"Is he in jail or what?"

"He's been placed out of town. He lived on the streets. His mother was a crack head and he never knew his father. He dropped out of school before he were a teenager. Nobody cared."

"Where is he now?"

"He's in a better place out in the country."

My cell phone buzzed. It was Detective Rank. "Good news. We picked up Ralph Mastroni this morning. And, a new trial date was set for next Thursday, 10:00 AM, at the courthouse at 2700 Tulane Avenue."

Chapter 36

9:00 AM, Sunday, August 24th

I was eating French toast and chicken at the Spotted Dog. Anthony Scala was singing with his guitarist.

> *"Some enchanted evening you may see a stranger,*
> *You may see a stranger across a crowded room,*
> *And somehow you know, you know even then...."*

"Hey Stretch. Hello. Hello. Come back to earth," said Benny, sitting across from me in the booth. He looked rather ruddy, like he was drinking a gin and tonic instead of coffee. I leaned over to see that it was actually dark coffee.

I shook my head and said, "Sorry about that. How long have you been here?"

He chuckled, "Well, I just popped in."

"That song just made me think of Carlotta. I've got to find her."

"You'll find her. You're getting closer."

165

I looked at him. "You know, don't you? You know where she is. Tell me. Please tell me. I've got to find her."

"She's not here, but there." He pointed towards the corner only upward.

I looked outside and said, "Where? Where outside?"

He began fading away. The couple in the table next to me looked at me strangely. I could barely see him, but I heard his last words, "She's out in the country at an old place. It's real old."

He was gone. So was his coffee cup. I smiled at the couple next to me. "Don't mind me. I'm working on the words for a novel that I'm writing." *Then it hit me. I understood why he was so vague. Although he was a ghost, Benny wasn't from here. He wasn't familiar with New Orleans. He had never lived here.*

Anthony sang the final stanza of the Rodgers and Hammerstein song.

"Who can explain it, who can tell you why?
Fools give you reasons, wise men never try.
Some enchanted evening you will find your true love,
You will find Carlotta in a crowded room,
Then fly to her side and take her home,
Or all through your life you may dream all alone,
Go now and find her and never let her go,
Go now and find her and never, ever let her go."

166

My fork dropped out of my hand and clanged on the floor. The lyrics blew me away. *"You will find Carlotta…. Go now and find her and never let her go."* I stood up and walked up to Anthony, but he was turned around talking to his guitarist, so I put a ten in the tip jar and walked back to the table. The server picked up the fork and asked, "Can I get you anything else?"

"No, No. I've gotta go now. I've gotta find someone. Can I have the check?"

A few minutes later he returned and set the check on the table. Without looking at it I handed him a twenty and left. *The message was clear what I had to do. Go now and find her and never, ever let her go.*

Chapter 37

12:00 PM

I walked down to Jackson Square to look for Madam Sherry. It was crowded. People were milling around the artists, musicians, and hucksters. A man wearing a white paper hat leaned over the Lucky Dog wagon surveying the crowd. People dressed up in suits and long dresses were filing out of St. Louis cathedral. Sunday Mass had ended.

There was no Madam Sherry. I walked back and forth scanning the crowd, focusing on the card readers, Mediums, musicians and entertainers that were sitting at tables. I really needed to talk to her. I was frustrated.

I sat down on a bench next to a man wearing an old torn shirt and tan, dirty jeans. He was sleeping with his head hung down on his chest, oblivious to the buzzing crowd of people walking by. A semitrailer truck rumbled around the corner of Chartres and St. Peter and stopped. It was a funny sight because the French Quarter streets were not

169

designed for large vehicles. Sure enough, he couldn't make the turn. The driver inched it back and forth but couldn't clear the corner. He jumped out and walked around the truck, trying to figure out how he could get out of the mess he was in. He couldn't back up because of the cars behind him. A pillar barricade prevented him from straightening out. After talking to people standing by, he got back in and plowed over two of the concrete bollards smashing them to bits. A woman screamed. The driver jumped out and spoke to a police officer who was writing down the truck license plate number on a ticket. Tourists were buzzing around the truck like bees, holding up their phones taking pictures.

The woman's scream woke up the man next to me. He raised his head and looked at the truck and muttered "dumb shit." Then he looked at me with his eyes still shut and said quite clearly, "You can find Madam Sherry at the big house tonight on Valley Road. Eleven o'clock."

I looked at him, but he hung his head down sound asleep.

Chapter 38

11:00 PM

When I got out of the car, I stepped into a puddle soaking my right foot. It was raining heavily. I opened an umbrella and held it over my head as I stepped carefully around the live oak branches that were guarding the house. I knocked on the door hard as I could to be heard above the pounding rain.

The door opened a crack and a brown robed person asked what I wanted. "I'm here to see Madam Sherry."

Bingo. Those were the magic words that opened the door wide enough to allow me to squeeze in. I set the umbrella down and followed the person toward the back courtyard. This time we stopped in a room where I was instructed to change into a brown hooded robe and put my clothes in a bag. The person said tonight was a special celebration. I changed clothes and felt like a clone as I followed him into the courtyard.

The courtyard was dark with the only light coming from flickering gas torches. A clay goblet was given to me. I sipped and tasted the same coconut rum drink that I had before. I walked around looking at faces hoping to find Carlotta. I counted about sixty people *but didn't see her.* There were five people sitting with their hooded heads hung down over two foot tall wood drums. They started hitting the gray leather tops with their fists. The drumming was loud and powerful as it vibrated off the walls and floor. I moved slowly through the crowd trying to find her. It seemed like a secret society, as people turned away or lowered their heads when I looked at them. Identities seemed highly guarded. The droopy hoods and bulky robes did a good job of masquerading people.

This time it was different. When the drumming slowed down people started chanting. I couldn't understand the words. It was a foreign language or different tongue.

"Ade Due damballa,
Give me the power I beg of you. I beg of you Laveau
mercier du bois charlotte.
Secoise entienne mais pois de morete. Ade Due
Damballa! Awake!"

The crowd chanted these words over and over, blending in with the drum beats. Suddenly the drums stopped. Everyone bowed their heads. A single person walked into the center of the ring and dropped her hood. It was Madam Sherry. This time she spoke in a loud, deep, clear voice:

> *"Ade Due damballa,*
> *Give me the power I beg of you Laveau mercier*
> *du bois chaloitte.*
> *Secoise entienne mais pois de morete. Mortiesma*
> *lieu de voicier de mieu vochette. Endenlieu pour*
> *du boisette Damballa.*
> *Endenlieu pour du boisette Damballa.*
> *Endenlieu pour boisette Damballa!*

A robed person walked up to Madam Sherry and lifted her robe off and carried it away into the crowd. All eyes were on her naked body as another robed person handed her a machete and rooster with its wings flapping wildly. She held the bird high in the air just as she had done before, and slowly turned around to show everyone and then sliced its head off with one swing of the machete. Poof! The headless bird dropped to the ground. She raised its head above her and let the blood stream over her face and onto her breasts. Immediately, drums started beating faster and faster. She sucked the cock's head with blood coming out of the corners of her mouth. She spit the head out of her mouth and raised her hands in the air and started dancing around the courtyard.

173

I couldn't take my eyes off of her. This time she danced slowly around the crowd looking deeply at each person with her dark brown eyes. When she stood inches from me, she looked into my eyes. Our eyes locked. I lost my own thoughts and saw a different world in her eyes. It felt spiritual and timeless. I felt small but part of it. It felt like I was in another world. When she moved away, I swayed in rhythm with the others, humming and humming.

Chapter 39

12:00 PM, Monday, August 25th

I woke up freezing in bed, butt naked. My mouth felt parched so I licked my lips over and over and sat up thinking about what happened last night. It wasn't only my lips that were numb. I had no feeling in my legs.

Was it just a dream or was I at that house again? I don't remember the ending. How did I get home? I didn't learn anything new about Carlotta. I didn't see her. Why did I go there? I don't remember talking to Madam Sherry. But that look in her eyes was so deep, so penetrating. What's going on? Then, I remembered the strange, spiritual connection that I felt from her.

I slumped back down and curled up under the sheet. I felt a weird sensation that my body and mind were separate.

My mind wanted to continue thinking about the night even though I couldn't remember all of it. It wanted to return.

My body felt cold. I couldn't feel my legs. I rubbed them and pushed them out of bed. Finally, I stood and walked into the living room.

Greg was sitting in my chair.

"Good morning, Greg."

"Thought you were going to sleep all day. Were you out late last night?"

"Yeah. I was out late." I didn't feel like telling him where I was. Hell, he's a ghost. He probably already knows where I was. I felt cold, tired, and not very talkative. Greg wasn't a big talker either. So the two of us sat in silence.

Finally, I said, "Greg, I was trying to find Carlotta last night. Somehow I think Madam Sherry is the key to help me find her. She's talked to her. She's seen her. I was at that old house on Valley Road last night. It's hard to describe what went on, but people were chanting while Madam Sherry danced. I felt like I was in another world. I had hoped to see Carlotta there. I looked and looked but didn't see her."

"Don't give up. Don't ever give up."

"Greg, why do I feel so cold? I'm freezing."

He looked at me and said, "It would help if you got dressed."

***

I walked down to Jackson Square and scanned the crowd for Madam Sherry, but she wasn't there.

I felt disappointed at not seeing her and decided to walk home past the mules waiting for tours and do a bit of window shopping on Decatur while enjoying the sunshine a little longer. I saw the brown spotted mule pulling a carriage full of tourists down Decatur Street. I overheard the tour guide talking about ghosts that haunted an old building as the carriage passed by.

I looked in shop and club windows as I walked. Then it struck me, that there weren't as many homeless people sitting on the sidewalks. I crossed the neutral ground on Esplanade and didn't see any gutter punks or train hoppers. As I walked further I saw orange spray paint and markers on several cracked sidewalks. Apparently the city planned to repair them.

**

When I was a block away from my house, I saw Greg sitting on the stoop. Instead of heading home, I turned into Buffa's for a cold beer. Benny was sitting alone in the corner.

"Hey Stretch, how's it going?"

"Good. Just went for a nice walk."

"No, ya didn't. You're still trying to find Carlotta aren't you?"

I looked at him, remembering that as a ghost he knows what I'm doing. Candy the bartender came over and asked, "Hey Bruce, were you speaking to me?"

"Yeah. I just went for a nice walk."

She set a cold Abita Amber in front of me, smiled and walked away.

I turned to look at Benny and said, "Yeah. I'm trying to find her. Now, that I know she's alive, I can't give up. I've gotta find her. I just don't know where she is."

Candy set the beer in front of me and gave me an odd look.

I sipped the beer and was going to continue talking to Benny, but waited until Candy started talking to a guy at the other end of the bar.

"Benny, can you help me find her?"

"Yeah. Sure, but you know I never lived here so I don't know how much I can help. Let me find out a few things and get back to you." He was gone.

Candy saw me talking to myself, came over and insisted that I pay for the beer. I dug out a ten dollar bill and set it on the bar. "Keep the change."

She gave me a funny look, took the money, and walked away.

Chapter 40

8:00 AM, Tuesday, August 26th

My phone buzzed on the nightstand. I was awake anyway and grabbed it. "Hello."

"Bruce this is Detective Rank. The Assistant District Attorney wants you to come down here for pre-trial prep for the Ralph Mastroni murder case. Since you're the key witness on Thursday, he wants to discuss your testimony. Can you be here by 9:00 AM?"

"Well, yah, sure. I'll be there. Where do I meet him?"

"Just come to the station. He's in my office now."

"OK."

I woke up relaxed, but, the phone call set my nerves on fire. I'd been thinking more about finding Carlotta than about the Barracks Street murder trial. I had felt so relieved that there would be no trial for Leo's killers since they admitted their guilt and were sentenced. And, thanks to Rocky

179

(and "the man"), the "hit" was cancelled and no one that I knew of was trying to kill me.

I hadn't forgotten the trial, but, hadn't worried about it until now. I started shaking thinking about testifying as a key witness to send someone to a life sentence or the death chamber.

Thank God the police had kept their word and withheld my name from the press.

I showered. Dressed in long pants and collared shirt and started the trek to the police station. Sunglasses and a cap made me feel less conspicuous.

**

"Paul this is ADA Arnold Jeffers." He offered me his hand and cracked a smile. He had brown eyes, dark wavy hair, mustache and full beard. His sharp nose made him look birdlike, tilting his head, and looking at me as if I were a big worm

"Please sit down," he said, as he put his hand on the chair across from him.

I looked at Rank and then back at the bird man. "Thank you."

"I want to walk you through what's going to happen Thursday in court. The accused defendant is Ralph Mastroni. He's got a long record of brutality and violence including rape and assault beating up women. Over the years he's served time in six states including Louisiana. Facing a murder one charge will put him away for good."

My mind drifted as I watched his lips move. I just wanted out. I wanted this whole situation to be over. It was a bad dream.

"Are you listening to me? Do you hear me?"

He must have seen the faraway look in my eyes. "Yes, I hear you."

"Ok. Let's start. Here's the first question that I'll ask you after you're sworn in on stand."

***

3 hours later

I was sitting at Buffa's clutching a cold beer. There was only one other person at the far end of the bar. Donny was working behind the bar. Without asking, he saw me guzzling and set another Abita Amber in front of me. "Geez, I feel sorry for you, man. First, losing your wife and now testifying in a murder trial. Life sucks, man."

I rubbed my fingers around the beer bottle, as if I was trying to squeeze the beer out. I told him about the three hour drilling I had from the ADA. Now, I felt totally drained. I slugged the beer down and slammed it on the bar.

"Please give me another, Donnie."

"This one's on me."

181

I nodded in thanks and took a long sip. "What's the problem? You'll be OK. Don't worry," Benny said from the corner bar stool.

I looked over at him. He had a sly grin on his face. "I mean it, don't worry. You'll be OK."

"That's what Greg says. That it'll be OK. HOW DO YOU KNOW THAT?" I screamed. Donnie and the guy he was talking to at the end of the bar looked at me.

Donnie walked over. "Are you alright, man? Maybe you should go back to your place and take a break."

I put a twenty on the bar and stood up, looked over at Benny and whispered "How do you know?"

He nodded his head up and down. "Trust me, it'll be OK."

I walked out the door and peeked in the front window of the bar, and saw Donnie talking to the guy at the far end. All the other bar stools were empty.

***

I fell asleep within seconds of lying down. I dreamt about Madam Sherry dancing naked. Her shiny naked body, breasts and hips were so tantalizing. *No. No. I thought, I don't want to go there. I love Carlotta. I don't wanna have sex with anyone else. I have to find Carlotta. I'm wasting too much time. I've gotta find Carlotta. I have to bring her home. She needs me.* I cried and woke up in a cold sweat. I'd been asleep for less than an hour. Sometimes the shorter dreams are the most realistic. My cell phone buzzed. It was Rocky. "I'll be over in a few minutes."

***

He knocked on the door three minutes later.

"Hey. What's happening?"

"That's what I want to ask you. What's new?"

"Well I got prepped today by the ADA for the trial Thursday. I'm getting nervous."

"Nervous about what? The boys are going to leave you alone. Sam gave his word!"

"Still, I'm the key witness testifying against a killer."

"Tell you what, I'll be there for you. In fact, I'll do even better than that. I'll pick you up in my cab and drive you to the courthouse."

"Thanks."

Chapter 41

1:30 AM, Thursday, August 28th

I had trouble falling asleep because of the trial. I opened the window and saw the stars sparkling like diamonds surrounding the full moon. It seemed so big that I could see shapes in it. I squinted to see what they were. The best I could do was a big collie dog. The same dog I saw as a kid. My mind drifted back to the trial and my testimony and what the defendant's attorney would ask me.

Then I rolled over and wondered what Carlotta was doing. *Was she really alive? Where is she?*

My mind wouldn't stop replaying what happened that night. I thought how scared I felt that night when she never came home. How I checked every club up and down Frenchman Street looking for her. How I didn't sleep that night, as I waited for the sound of her key in the door.

The next morning I starting calling her friends, but got frustrated when I realized I didn't know their last names or have their phone numbers. Carlotta was a good friend to others, she was fun to be with and made people

185

feel good, so her list of friends was a mile long. But I didn't have the list.

I didn't call the police because I still thought she was OK, just stayed out overnight, perhaps drank too much, and fell asleep at a friend's place. I'd give her hell the next day when she came home for not calling me.

She had stayed out late before and always came home. However, this was the first time that she didn't come home. When she didn't return the next day, I phoned the police to report her missing. I told them about her love for music and how she would walk down to Frenchman Street to listen to live music several days a week. That's what she did. She loved New Orleans energy and its people and wanted to actively participate in it through its music and food.

She just didn't come home. Sure, they gave me a hard look to see if I had done something to her, but were finally convinced that my story was true.

My eyes were open. I couldn't sleep. After the weeks turned into months, I was a mess. I didn't give up but didn't know what to do. I felt broken.

My life's been Hell since. Now, I'm a witness in a murder trial. I rolled over on my side with my head buried in the pillow and closed my eyes. I pulled the sheets up to my neck. I felt cold.

Chapter 42

10:00 AM,
District Courthouse, New Orleans, LA

Perspiration soaked my collar. I wore a suit and tie for the first time since I attended my father's funeral. It was eighty one degrees and climbing. The AC and the whirling ceiling fans in the crowded court room were fighting a losing battle to cool the air as sweat kept streaming out of me. I felt that I was melting. People sitting behind me were fanning themselves.

A man in a uniform yelled out, "EVERYBODY. PLEASE RISE FOR THE HONORABLE JUDGE ELIJAH JANE THOMPSON." A middle aged woman wearing a long black robe walked out and sat down behind the large elevated wooden desk. Everyone sat down after she sat down.

The ADA and the defense attorney stood up to tell the judge their stories of what happened.

And then I heard my name called. My mouth felt like I had just eaten a dozen cotton balls. I sat down in the chair next to the judge. I could hardly say "I will" after I was sworn in to "tell the truth, the whole truth and nothing but the truth."

ADA Jeffers approached me and asked "Please state your name for the court."

"Bruce Paul."

"Mr. Paul please tell us what happened?"

I looked at the ADA then looked over at the defendant and his attorney. I cleared my throat and said, "I was walking down Barracks Street at about ten o'clock in the morning on Monday, July 8th. I was looking down at the cracked sidewalks because they were bad in that block. When I looked over at the shotgun houses across the street, I heard fighting and loud screaming and yelling. I stood frozen not knowing what to do. The front door of the house where the fighting was burst open and a man stumbled down the stoop, got up fast and ran around the corner."

The ADA asked, "Is that man present in the court room this morning?"

"Yes Sir."

"Please point him out for the record."

"He's sitting right there." I pointed at the defendant.

The defendant shook his head and glared at me. Then he held up his hand as if it were a gun, aimed at me and pulled the trigger.

I looked at the Jury to see if they saw him.

The ADA walked towards me. "Please, tell the court what happened next."

"I waited a few minutes to see if he was coming back. Then I crossed the street and walked up the stoop to look through the opened door way." I looked at the people in the jury who were all looking at me.

"Yes, please continue."

"I saw a woman lying on the floor with her face down in the middle of the living room. She wasn't moving so I walked inside and knelt down to see if she was breathing. Then I checked her pulse by holding her wrist."

"Did you find one?"

"There was no pulse. She was dead."

"What else?"

"I saw black marks around her neck and bruises on her face."

"Then what did you do?"

"I called 911. Then I closed the door and sat down on the front stoop to wait for the police."

"Thank you Mr. Paul. Oh, wait, I have one more question. Do you see the person that ran out of the house in the courtroom?"

I was confused because I had already answered this question. I didn't know why he asked me a second time. But, I knew it didn't make sense to argue. I answered "Yes Sir, it's the defendant sitting there." I pointed at him with my finger.

"Are you positive?"

"Yes Sir."

"Thank you."

This time the defendant motioned with his hand that he would slash my neck. I quickly looked at the Jury to see that most of them saw the threat.

The defendant's attorney, a rat-looking man dressed in a brown suit jumped up. He had dark beady eyes with a thin mustache and long pointy nose. He yelled as if I were deaf, "Mr. Paul, did you say that you saw the defendant hit the deceased?"

"No Sir. I did not."

"You did not what? "

"I did not see him hit her."

"Did you see him strike her or even squeeze her neck?"

"No Sir. I did not."

"You did not what?"

"I did not see him strike her or squeeze her neck."

"So you really don't know if the defendant, this man, was the murderer, do you?"

ADA Jeffers jumped up. "Objection. "Your honor, the defendant's counsel is drawing a conclusion for the witness."

"Sustained. The jury will disregard counsel's last statement."

The defendant's attorney threw his hands in the air, shrugged his shoulders, and sat down. "I have no further questions of this witness your Honor."

The judge told me that I could step down. I walked towards ADA Jeffers. He asked me to stay in the building in case I am called again.

***

At twelve thirty, the courtroom doors opened and people burst out. ADA Jeffers saw me sitting on a wood bench facing the door way and walked over. "Thanks for your testimony. You did a good job."

"Thanks. Can I leave now?"

"No. There's a chance you might be called back. The judge said the trial will reconvene at two o'clock. Just remember, if you're called back in, just tell the truth and keep your answers short."

Rats, I thought to myself, I wanted to get out of there. Jeffers added, "Hey the trial's going well. It wouldn't surprise me if it goes to the Jury by five. Once it goes to the Jury, you're free to leave."

Chapter 43

5:30 PM

I was sitting at Cosimo's talking to Rocky and Benny. There was a Shetland sheepdog sitting on the stool next to Benny.

Cosimo's was an old bar with a lot of history. Years ago, like 60-70 years ago, New Orleans Mafia hung out there. People such as Carlos Marcello, Lee Harvey Oswald, Kent "Frenchie" Brouillette, Clay Shaw and other colorful characters were frequent customers. In fact, Frenchie told me in an interview for a book that Carlos Marcello was so upset with the Kennedys for deporting him to South America that he swore a vendetta against them. Frenchie said that he and Oswald were twenty one years old at the time and did errands for Mr. Marcello. He chuckled and said he was glad that he wasn't asked to knock off Kennedy. Oswald was given the task. The rest is history. Today, Cosimo's is a quiet, local watering hole.

I sipped on a cold Abita Amber.

"I felt like I was the one on trial."

193

Benny reached out and patted me on the back. "You did OK. I told you, it'd be OK."

"Thanks," I said, rubbing the beer bottle.

Rocky said, "Who the hell are you talking to? Me, the friggin' dog or the empty bar stool?"

I remembered that Rocky can't see him. "I'm worn out from the court room. It feels like being put through a wringer. The defense attorney tried to twist my words and imply that I didn't see anything."

"You did alright."

I looked at Benny, but remembered Rocky can't see him so I turned to tell Rocky.

"I'm just tired. Don't mind me. It's cold in here, isn't it?"

"Hey, you did OK in there. I saw the whole thing. You did fine."

"ADA Jeffers did a good job preparing me. He told me to answer the questions truthfully and briefly. He emphasized briefly, meaning to say as few words as possible."

"That makes good sense. You're not up there to win an award"

"Thanks for driving me and being there, Rocky. I felt nervous and couldn't wait to get out of there. Waiting afterwards, expecting to get called back in the afternoon, drove me crazy."

"Hey. All's well that ends well. The Jury didn't waste any time finding him guilty of second degree murder. That dude's gonna be locked up for a long time."

I raised the empty beer bottle to signal the bartender for another. I took a deep breath and looked out the window at the people walking by. "And so it goes," as Kurt Vonnegut often wrote.

Chapter 44

7:00 PM, Friday, August 29th

I was invited by good friends, Janet and Bert, to attend a birthday party for their dog Ruby that night at their beautiful historic home across from Cabrini Park. There were about 30 people at the party. A young man wearing a tuxedo played soft jazz on their jet black Steinway grand piano in the parlor. Once everyone had eaten and was on their second or third glass of wine, they gathered around the piano to listen closer. He had an excellent voice and knew how to play just about every song request. Wine, music, and good people make the world go round I thought. The party helped me wash away the stress from the trial. He sang one of my songs that I had written a few years ago.

> *"Hey dizzy, dizzy, dizzy Miss Lizzie,*
> *Please kiss, kiss, kiss, kiss me.*
> *I feel like a frog,*
> *Living in a bog,*
> *Until I met you, now I feel cool!"*

***

I walked home alone at ten. It felt good that no one at the party asked about Carlotta. Although it was almost a year since she left, I still felt like "a half couple" around "couple friends." *The look in their eyes made me feel sad and helpless that I should be doing more to find her. That I didn't deserve to have fun without her.*

I lay awake thinking about her. We had so much fun together. I missed her so much.

I wondered what happened to her… every… single… day. I felt good knowing that she's alive. But is she really alive? Or does she exist in a different life? I was frustrated knowing she wants to come home, but can't. I don't understand why she can't come home. Is she being held prisoner? I have to find her. I just have to find her. I fell asleep repeating "I have to find her" a hundred times. I felt cold.

***

I thought about Madam Sherry's eyes. They were so deep and mysterious. Then I fell asleep and dreamt during the night that… *I was standing in the front yard of a large plantation home in the country. It had yellow painted siding with ten thick white columns in the front of the house. There was a big porch with four large white painted rocking chairs on each side of the double black front door. In the corner was a white wicker table and six chairs. There was a woman sitting at the table drinking coffee or tea from a delicate looking white china cup. I saw crackers on a dish on the table.*

A man strode out of the doorway yelling at someone as he left. "It better be goddamned ready when I get back, ya hear?" Then he sat down in a chair next to the woman.

She asked him, "What's wrong dear? Is the new girl not working out?"

His eyes were dark and strong as he turned to look at her and said, "She's like all the rest. Can hardly speak English. How hard can it be to fill up the tub with hot water?"

There were chickens walking with their heads bobbing up and down eating insects and seeds. A woman wearing a big white apron carried a basket and hung up clothes to dry on the long rope tied between two trees on the side of the house. It was a good day for it, since the breeze was steady, blowing the Spanish moss dangling from the live oaks. A man rode up with a mule pulling a wagon. There was a big pile of cut sugar cane stacked in the wagon. He jumped off the wagon when he got to an old building behind the house. Two young men walked out to meet him. The three of them grabbed armfuls of the cane and carried it inside the building. It was a working plantation. People were busy. No one was talking though. There was no one playing. No one laughing. I turned my attention back to the couple on

199

the front porch. They were silent and looking away from each other.

I woke up thinking about the dream. Was the plantation the same one that I had visited with Barry and Carla? *Why did I dream about it? What does it mean?*

Chapter 45

10:00 AM, Saturday, August 30th

I woke up, showered, dressed, and walked down Esplanade. My plan was to find out from Madam Sherry where Carlotta was. I didn't see her at the parties or gatherings. She was supposed to be there, but, I didn't see her. I was frustrated and felt stuck in my search. I figured that Madam Sherry was the key.

She was sitting at her table, wearing the same deep red head wrap. She didn't see me approach, so I cleared my throat. "Ahem. Madam Sherry."

She looked up. "Good morning. How can I help you?"

I was surprised that she didn't recognize me. Maybe she was blinded by the light. "I'm still trying to find my wife. I need your help."

She blinked three times. Her dark eyes pierced through me. After ten seconds, she looked at me more softly, "I'm sorry baby. Of course I remember you. You're Tom, right?

"No. I'm…"

She interrupted me, "No, I mean Bruce. You're Bruce, right?"

"Yes, I'm Bruce." After I said that, it dawned on me that I never really told her my name. My focus had been entirely on my wife. And, without me telling her, she knew her names, Carlotta and Bunny.

"She was there, you know. She was at the parties. That's why I wanted you to come."

I was startled. "But I didn't see her. I didn't see her. Everyone wore hoods. It was dark and hard to see faces." Now I felt frustrated learning that she was there.

"CAN YOU PLEASE TELL ME WHERE SHE IS NOW?" I blurted out.

She didn't say anything as she removed a white cloth exposing a crystal ball on the table in front of her. She bowed her head and peered into it. I watched her carefully as her eyes moved as though she was seeing something inside the ball. Finally, she spoke without taking her eyes off the crystal ball. "I see a woman. She has dark reddish brown hair. It seems redder in the sunlight. It's your wife. She is carrying a pail of water. There are others crouching down in a garden. They're picking weeds and tossing them in a pile. No one is speaking. I see a man on a horse. The horse is dark, maybe black, with a white spot on its head and dark brown saddle. This horse is shiny. The man has a straw hat with a black bandana wrapped around it. He's holding a leather whip in his right hand. There's a gun. It's a rifle in the saddle. The man's yelling. He's screaming at the people. I can't understand what he's saying. He looks mean. He's very angry."

Suddenly, she slumps downward. Her head hung, spiritless, her chin to her chest, with her mouth open. It was if she had seen a ghost or some supernatural force. I had heard that people with such special gifts get drained and suffer health problems. I sat and waited. After a few minutes she perked up. Her head jerked straight up. She looked at me as though she saw me for the first time and said slowly "Your wife's being held captive at this place. It's an old cane plantation out in the country. She can't leave."

Chapter 46

2:00 AM, Sunday, August 31st

I fell asleep thinking about Madam Sherry's seeing Carlotta at an old plantation that afternoon. I dreamt about her...

She was bent over in a garden with other people, pulling carrots and greens out and tossing them in a straw basket. Her hands were dirty. She wore a dark sack dress. It was a big garden, maybe a couple hundred feet by fifty feet wide. A big planation style house shadowed it. Everything seemed black and white. There was no color. There was no sound.

I woke up, but didn't want the dream to end, so I squeezed my eyes shut to return to the site. It seemed that she was caught or stuck in a time warp. It seemed like a different world, a different time. The dream continued...

She turned her head and looked at me as though she could see me. She cried out, but I couldn't hear her. I watched her closely. She was begging for help. She was crying. I could see tears running down her face. I yelled out. I'M HERE. I'M HERE.WHERE ARE YOU?

WHERE ARE YOU? I'LL COME AND GET YOU.
Then my mind went blank. I opened my eyes and
sat up.

Chapter 47

12:30 PM

"You've gotta quit drinking. Man, you're losin' it," said Rocky.

I told him about my last meeting with Madam Sherry and my dream. I rubbed my forehead and then my eyes. "She's being held captive on a plantation."

"Madam Sherry told you this?"

"Yeah. She's seen her and communicated with her."

"You believe her?"

"Yeah, I do. Madam Sherry has special powers. I don't understand it, but she is able to connect. She can see things. I believe in her."

Rocky looked at me. "I've been hearing that for years, but never really believed it."

The dream I had last night seemed more like a vision. Carlotta was working at a plantation like a slave. It seemed like it was back in time. It's like she's trapped in a time warp and can't escape."

Rocky chewed on his cigar so much that the top half fell on the bar. He swept the cigar and tobacco crumbs on the floor and then said, "I've got an idea."

Chapter 48

3:00 PM, Monday, September 1st

Rocky and I picked up Madam Sherry from her table in front of the cathedral. It was raining so she sat under an umbrella without any customers. We told her we needed her to show us the plantation where she saw Carlotta working. Although she resisted at first, Rocky told her that she didn't have a choice. Madam Sherry's niece stood nearby and walked over. "Go ahead. Help them. I'll take care of your business."

Rocky, Madam Sherry, and I drove over the Destrehan/Luling Bridge and turned on highway 3127. After twenty three miles we turned onto highway 20 to highway 18 to River Road going towards Vacherie, a small town with a population of 2,400 in St. James Parish. Vacherie is a Cajun French term for "cattle fields."

There was a lot of scrubby woods, fields, and scattered housing as we drove in Rocky's taxi van. Oh, I forgot to mention that Benny and Greg were in the back seat, unknown to Rocky, who couldn't see them in the rearview mirror.

Greg said softly as if he didn't want Rocky to hear. "I don't really like these old plantations. They make me feel creepy. Too many bad spirits. Too much sadness."

Benny responded, "That's long gone. Times are different today. Don't worry about it. All we've gotta do is find Bruce's wife, grab her, and drive like hell outta there."

"Right," I added, agreeing with Benny.

Rocky said, "You want me to turn right? Where?"

"It's about a mile ahead," said Madam Sherry. Then she added, "There are a lot of spirits that are still around from the slaves that worked on the plantations. Lots of them are buried there. I don't like going there either."

I thought it was eerie that Madam Sherry heard Greg and Benny speak. Rocky turned his head around like an owl with a cigar in his mouth and said to Madam Sherry, "Just show us where Carlotta is."

"The plantation's around the next curve. Slow down and turn right on the next road," she said.

An old wood sign with painted brown letters "L A N D R Y" marked the dirt road leading off the highway. Rocky slowed down, turned the lights off, and drove slowly so we could sneak in. It felt like we were entering Jurassic Park only this place had a different theme, like a sugar cane plantation in the 1800s. There were no trucks or cars. Only a stable of mules and a horse, a dark black horse.

It was quiet. Too quiet. We got out and carefully nudged the van doors shut. A tall man dressed in a pressed white shirt, black suspenders, dark brown pants and black boots stepped out onto the veranda. It may have been his handle bar mustache and dark eye brows that made him look mean. He had a long knife in a sheath on his left leg and a pistol in a holster on his right side. He took two steps forward and stared at us. When he didn't speak, the four of us walked towards him. Madam Sherry stayed behind in the van feeling uneasy.

He stared at each of us, one at a time. I thought it was odd for him to look at not only Rocky and me, but also at Greg and Benny. *How could he see them? Was he also a ghost?*

"WHAT THE HELL DO YOU WANT?"

Rocky spoke first. "We heard about this place. Just thought we'd stop to see how the work is coming along. When will you be open for tourists?"

The man thought about what Rocky said and replied, "I'm Jacque Landry, the owner of this plantation. There's still a lot of work that needs to be done before we'll allow tourists. It'll be a while."

"Can we look around?" I asked.

"You look familiar. Have I seen you before?"

"No," I lied. Knowing this was the plantation that I stopped at with Carla and Barry.

211

"We do not give tours. And we don't want people walking around disturbing my workers. Please leave,"

We ignored him and started walking around the side of the house. Landry stepped off the porch, shot his pistol in the air and yelled "ENOUGH! GET THE HELL OUT OF HERE! NOW!"

The shot got our attention as we raised our arms. I said, "OK. OK, WE'RE LEAVING."

"He's hiding something." Benny said.

"He doesn't want us to see the people." Greg said.

"How can he see Benny and Greg?" I asked.

Rocky looked at me funny. "Who are Benny and Greg?"

Benny answered, "Landry can see us because he's a ghost."

Greg nodded. "Yeah. He's a ghost. He's a mean evil ghost. Let's get outta here."

"This is weird." I said.

Rocky nodded. "And it's getting weirder."

The four of us got in the van. We told Madam Sherry what happened. But she already knew.

She said, "People used to think I was crazy when I told them I can see spirits. There are plenty of spirits at this place. It gives me the creeps."

Greg replied, "Me too. I don't like this place."

"Carlotta's there," Madam Sherry said. "I feel it. She's there."

While Landry watched, Rocky backed out and drove out on the dirt road. Before we got to the highway, I said, "Stop! I've got an idea."

Rocky parked the van, and we walked single file through the head-high sugar cane just far enough from the driveway so we could follow it, but stayed hidden from view. When we got close enough to see the house, we knelt down to watch. Benny put his hand on my shoulder and pointed at three women dressed in brown sack dresses weeding the garden.

"Is one of them her?" I asked.

Benny said, "No. I thought so at first, but I was wrong."

We crouched down and watched the house. Landry stepped out and walked over to the left of the veranda. I looked to see that he was watching the women bending over in the garden. He walked back on the veranda towards the door. A woman stepped out and greeted him. They walked to the corner and sat down at a table. A woman wearing a white apron brought out a tray with a pitcher and two porcelain cups. She set it down and poured its contents into their cups. It looked like tea.

We were too far away to hear what they were saying to each other. It looked like a scene from "Gone with the Wind". The whole scene seemed to be from a period of time way back. Suddenly, Landry jumped up, and ran over to the center of the veranda and down the steps. He yelled at a

213

teenage boy who was talking to one of the women in the garden. The boy cowered, bending his head down as Landry approached and struck him with the long leather whip which seemed to have spurs tied to its long tip. The whip wrapped around the boy's neck choking him. When Landry pulled back, the boy fell to the ground, gagging.

Three young men riding in a wagon with large wood wheels pulled by two mules drove around the house. The wagon was filled with sugar cane. Landry dropped the whip and yelled "YOU'RE LATE. GOD DAMMIT. WHERE'VE YOU BEEN?"

"Sorry Master. Sorry. The wagon tipped over in the ditch. We had to pick up the cane and put it back in."

"TAKE IT TO THE MILL, NOW! THEY'RE WAITING FOR YOU. GET MOVING, YA HEAR?"

The driver shook the reins and the mules trotted towards the tall building on the far side of the house. Landry sat back down next to the woman.

Rocky whispered to me, "This is nuts. These people are living like it was 200 years ago."

I nodded, "Let's get out of here." We stood up and walked quietly through the sugar cane to the highway.

Chapter 49

10:30 AM, Tuesday, September 2nd

"But you didn't actually see her," said Detective Rank.

"No. But, a friend told me she's there. She's working at that planation against her will and can't come home. I think she was kidnapped."

"Who's your friend?"

For some reason, I sensed a negative vibe and told him that I didn't want to share my friend's name.

He shook his head and laughed. "I think you're getting played. Who told you this? Was it some Medium or card reader?"

"I can't tell you."

I'm sorry but I can't do anything without hard evidence."

I was devastated.

Rank looked at me and said, "I need proof."

***

I drove over to the Fitness Center on St. Claude. Cap Black saw me park.

"Hey, Bruce, what's happening?"

"Hi Cap. Good to see you. I know where Carlotta is."

"Where?"

"She's being held captive on an old plantation on River Road." I explained to him that I reported it to the police but they didn't believe me.

"Hey man. Let's get her. I'll help."

***

12:00 midnight

Rocky, Cap, Benny, Greg and I dressed in black shirts and pants and drove out to River Road at midnight.

Stumbling through a Louisiana sugar cane field in the dark is the creepiest feeling I've ever experienced. Cap Black was in the lead. Since we didn't use flash lights to light our way for fear of alerting Landry, we were practically blind. So we followed behind each other closely. We could hear things moving out of our way. At least I liked to think they were moving away.

Rocky tripped, fell, and swore "Jesus H. Christ." I automatically responded "Shhhhh!" I reached for him and grabbed his shirt to pull him up. He whispered that his leg hurt. We plodded on. Benny and Greg had no trouble following behind us. They seemed to glide smoothly along. Rocky was breathing heavily. Enough for the five of us. No, there was six. There was a goat following Rocky.

We stopped when we neared the edge of the cane and saw dim lights in the house. "Sit down. Let's wait until our eyes adjust. We need visual purple." Cap whispered.

"Visual purple? I need oxygen," said Rocky, panting.

After sitting down a few minutes, I dozed off. It wasn't very long before I felt a tugging on my shirt sleeve. It was Cap. "Bruce. Bruce, wake up. We gotta move now. Let's go get her!"

I rubbed my eyes, squinted and looked out into the yard. We had walked further in the cane than I thought as were even with the big house and close to a string of small wood shacks.

I heard boards creaking as people were stirring and walking out of the shacks. I could hear talking. Two teenage boys walked over to a fire pit and started filling it with sticks. As the gray light increased I saw a woman moving further down from them. She wore a cream dress that looked like burlap. She was talking to another woman sitting on a small log bench. One of the boys tossed a lit match into the fire pit. Poof! It flamed up immediately. The second boy set a black steel grate over the fire. A woman walked over to set a coffee pot on the grate. She was dressed the same as the other women in a plain cream sack dress.

217

A woman walked out of another house with her arms stretched out carrying a basket of clothes. She walked over to the large black sugar kettle. It had to be at least six feet diameter. She took out a burlap sack like shirt, dipped it into the water and started squeezing and rubbing it clean. The lighter it became the more we could see. Chickens walked out of a house and started pecking the ground. A goat, no, there were three goats, walked around the woman with her head down washing the clothes. Suddenly, the goat next to Rocky, stepped on him, and trotted out of the cane to join the other goats. Rocky moaned. I held my finger over my mouth.

It looked like a village with people doing what they do every day. Rocky turned his head and whispered "Ya know what's wrong here?"

"No. What?"

"There aren't any old men. I mean full grown men. There are only women and young men. No old men."

"Those two boys look awfully familiar." I said.

There were at least twenty people milling about now. They were all dressed in cream or brown. It made it difficult to get an accurate head count. Rocky was right. I didn't see any old men.

"Whoa," I muttered, when I saw her. It was Carlotta. I knew it was her for sure when I saw the bunny tattoo on her right shoulder. She stood by the fire pit pouring coffee into a mug. After she placed the pot back on the grill, she took a sip and looked towards me. At least she looked at us. I couldn't tell if she actually saw me.

We were well hidden in the cane, but it seemed like the increasing daylight was exposing us more and more. Suddenly, everyone stopped doing what they were doing. All heads turned toward the big house.

Landry rode around the corner of the house on the black horse holding a whip in his right hand. Without warning, he whipped the closest young boy causing him to fall down and yelled "GIT UP, YA LAZY BONEHEAD!"

The kid was crying, but jumped up and stood straight. Landry yelled "WHAT YOU LOOKING AT, BOY?" Then he turned and yelled at the others "WHAT Y'ALL LOOKING AT? GIT TO WORK. CODDAMMIT GET TO WORK, YA LAZY BUNCH OF NO GOODS!"

Landry trotted slowly in front of the shacks, moving his head to look at each person. People hung their heads to avoid making eye contact until he rode away into the back field. As soon as he was out of sight, everyone returned to what they were doing. I snapped pictures of the people and zoomed in on Carlotta standing, walking, and kneeling by the sugar kettle.

"Let's get the hell out of here," Cap whispered.

"What about Carlotta?" I asked.

"Bruce you've found her. You've got plenty of pictures. It should be all the evidence the police need to shut this place down. Let's do it the right way and turn it over to the police."

Chapter 50

9:00 AM, Wednesday, September 3rd

Rocky picked me up because we thought we should both go down to the NOPD to meet with Detective Rank. I jumped in the van, but didn't shut the door. I left it open for Greg and Benny to climb into the back seat. One of them closed the door. Unless Rocky did, but I didn't see him hit the button. He turned around when it closed itself. "Damn door's acting up again. I've gotta get it fixed. It opens and closes by itself. Did it last night too."

I turned around and looked at Greg and Benny, who were laughing. I mouthed, "I wish he could see you guys."

Rocky looked at me out of the corner of his eye.

We parked in a taxi cab marked parking space across the street from the police station. Rank saw us walk in and waved us into his office.

"Please sit down."

"Thanks."

"You called and said you had something important. What you got?"

I was excited. I started talking too fast. "Whoa. Whoa. Slow down. Slow down."

I took a deep breath and said, "We drove out to the old Landry plantation on River Road last night. We hid in the cane field until it was gray light. We saw Carlotta. Yes, yes, she's there. I took pictures with my phone. Here's the proof."

I showed him the cell phone pictures of Carlotta pouring coffee, drinking coffee, looking at us, the zoomed in bunny tattoo on her shoulder, Landry on the horse whipping the young boy, the people with their heads down and Landry riding away.

Rank looked at us after handing me the phone back. "Send me these pics now."

I emailed the pics to him. He looked at them again on his lap top.

"OK. This is the evidence we needed. I will talk to my Captain. Stay here."

He carried the open lap top with him, shutting the door behind him. Benny walked around and sat in Rank's empty chair. Greg tipped the waste basket upside down and sat on it.

"Make yourselves at home," I said.

Rocky looked at me again out of the corner of his eye without turning his head. "Who're you talking to?"

"Hey. Hey. I was just kidding."

"I think it would have been better to tell Sam instead of the police about that place. He would saw the guy's legs off."

In a few minutes Rank walked back into the office. "Captain said that it'll be taken care of."

"What does that mean?"

"That means the police will handle it from this point on. We'll see that you get your wife back."

"When?"

He stood up and walked us toward the door. He put his hand on my shoulder and said, "We'll handle it. It's a police matter now. Let us do our work."

"Why do I feel stupid?" I asked Rocky on the way out.

Rocky raised his eyebrows and shook his head. "Because you are. No, I'm kidding. That's the way the police operate. They want you to tell them everything you know, but when you ask them a question, they don't tell you jack shit. Not even the time of day."

I had an empty feeling the rest of the day.

Chapter 51

3:00 PM

I was sitting at Buffa's just chilling out. There were five other people sitting at the bar. I was talking to Benny about the meeting with the police.

"Wonder when they'll bring Carlotta back?" I picked up my phone off the bar to check for messages.

"Well, you brought the police into it. Now it's complicated. We should've grabbed her when we had the chance. We could've done it. We were there."

"That's easy for you to say. But, what about the other people? There were at least thirty, probably more, that are being held captive."

I took a long swig from the cold bottle of Abita Amber.

Benny shook his head and said, "We should go back and snatch her. Who knows how long it'll take the police? Why wait? Let's bring her home. The police can rescue the others."

225

"Yeah. You're right. We blew it. We should have grabbed her. We were close. Cap thought we should do it the right way. He didn't want anyone getting hurt.

"I wonder when the police will go out there."

"It could be today, or this week, or this month, or whenever they get around to it," said Benny.

"Geez."

"Here's something else to think about. Landry's plantation is located way beyond the city limits. Heck, it's outside the Orleans Parish limits. It's in St. James Parish. I don't think NOPD has any jurisdiction there. Can they actually go out there?"

"God, you're not helpin'. You're making me feel worse."

"You asked a NOPD detective for help because you live in New Orleans. Your wife's a missing person from here."

"If it's out of NOPD's jurisdiction, why didn't he say that?" This question snatched my thoughts and threw them into a whirlpool. I squeezed my eyes and shook my head to clear them out like an etch-a-sketch. I guzzled the beer and set a ten on the bar.

***

I walked back and saw Greg sitting on the front stoop.

"What's happening?"

"All's good."

226

I walked in the house and felt a cold draft. Greg was now sitting in my chair.

"Geez. You scare the heck out of me. How'd you move so fast?"

He smiled and looked at me and said, "Since I'm a ghost, I weigh nothing and have no form, so I just think where I wanna be and I'm there."

I shook my head in amazement. I reached over to touch him and felt his arm. "How come I can see and touch you?"

"Because you're my friend and I'm your friend, and want you to know that I'm here." Greg had an aura around him as he spoke. His eyes looked large and all knowing.

"Can you be in more than one place at a time?"

"No. I'm only here now."

It may sound crazy, but I felt like I was talking to God. "Greg, can you do me a favor?"

"If it's a good thing you ask, I'll try my best."

"Can you go out to the Landry plantation to see if the police have been there yet? If they haven't been there, check to see if Carlotta is still there and get a head count how many people are working there. Greg, if they're prisoners or slaves, we need to help free all of them."

"Yes Sir."

"Greg, one more thing, please find out what shack Carlotta lives in. OK?"

Before I said "Thanks." He was gone. I mean, the chair was empty. I looked at the seat cushion and saw no impression where he sat. Sure, I had known that Greg was a ghost for some time, but I never thought too deeply about it until now. Knowing that he can disappear and reappear so fast, when he wants, made me think that he has super powers that will help me find her and bring her back.

I dosed off sitting on the sofa. I could fall asleep easily whether sitting or lying down. Just close my eyes and, voila! I enter the Land of Wink and Nod.

I enjoyed dreaming. It sure beats "circling" or staying awake feeling broken. *I'm dreaming now…. I see Greg and Benny crouched behind a palmetto watching the old plantation. I was surprised to see Benny with Greg. I guess the adage that "birds of a feather flock together' is true. In this case they were both ghosts; they were both looking through binoculars which seemed peculiar for ghosts, even for a dream.*

***

When I woke up, still sitting upright on the sofa, Benny and Greg were both sitting in my chair staring at me. I rubbed my eyes and asked "How long have you guys been here?"

I looked at my watch to see how long I'd been asleep. It was six o'clock.

Greg spoke first, "Just got here."

"What'd ya see?"

Greg said "I saw 4,593 people. That's counting all the men, women and children."

"No way. How can there be that many?" I asked.

Benny spoke up, "Let me explain what he means. He counted all the people living there since the plantation was built in 1817."

Greg nodded in agreement.

"OK, but what I really want to know is how many people live there now? Living people?"

"73," Greg answered.

"How many workers?"

Greg squinted his eyes and said "I'd say 68 work."

Benny chimed in. "Sixty eight work, but they aren't really employees because they aren't paid. They're allowed to eat the food they grow and the animals they raise. They sleep in the small shacks."

"They aren't allowed to leave the plantation. They work from dawn 'til dusk. They're captive."

"There's one more thing that you need to know." He looked at Greg and then back at me and said "Detective Rank and others at NOPD are in on it."

"What? I don't understand? What do you mean?"

"While we were there, Rank dropped off three young boys. They were handcuffed when he turned them over to Landry who chained them to a post in the front yard."

229

Greg said "Rank's friends with Landry. They sat down on the porch and smoked cigars together."

"We also saw Landry hand Rank a wad of cash."

Greg took a deep breath. "Here's what's going on. Have you noticed that you don't see many gutter punks, train hoppers, homeless, or bums slumming around on the neutral ground anymore? Remember how bad it was a few years ago?" There were dozens of people dressed in brown drab clothes sitting on the neutral ground and sidewalks on Decatur Street. And there were people begging at most street corners. Well, no longer. They're gone. The new Mayor pledged to clean up the streets and she meant it. She kept her promise by giving the police full authority to take whatever action necessary to make the city a safer place for its citizens and for tourists.

"She's had a blind eye since, not caring about what happens to them. She just wanted them gone off the streets. Rank and his cohorts pick them up off the streets and drop off the vagrants and juvies at Landry's plantation where they're forced into labor. Nobody really seems to care what happens to them. They're slave labor. They work for free."

I was shocked. "Really? Slave labor in today's way of life?"

Benny responded, "Yep. And it works. Everyone's happy, except for the vagrants and juvies who are forced to work to survive. The city's

230

considerably safer now. Shop owners are happier not having beggars blocking their doorways or harassing tourists. There's less crime and less litter in the city."

I thought about what he said. "But, it just isn't right? Slavery is wrong."

Greg said, "They've got a problem now. I mean the police. Somehow your wife got there by mistake. And, they know that you know about the place."

Chapter 52

3:00 AM, Thursday, September 4th

"She's in the fourth shack" whispered Greg, who seemed out of breath after his search to find Carlotta. He sounded breathy, "She's sleeping on the floor under the back window. But we gotta be careful 'cause there're seven other people asleep."

Cap Black, Rocky, Benny, Greg and I were crouched down in the edge of the cane watching the plantation. We could see the dim light from gas lanterns that were hung on spikes next to each door way. There was a dark shape of a man sleeping in a rocking chair on the veranda of the main house.

Rocky's cell phone lit up. "Geez. Turn that damn thing off." I whispered.

"It's in my pocket."

"Turn it off. The light shines through your pants."

Earlier in the afternoon, we had a group talk about the pros and cons of the Landry plantation. Our conclusion was that we understood why the police placed the gutter punks, train hoppers,

233

beggars, vagrants, and criminals there. It was an unofficial "prison camp" and they didn't want any publicity. We get it… that the city has too much vagrancy, and crime was out of control, but the Landry plantation was not a good solution. It was a step backward into painful southern history.

We decided not to wait for the police but to extract her tonight.

"OK," Cap said, "Here's the plan. Greg will go inside the fourth shack and open the door for us; Benny will watch the house for Landry or any guard. Whistle if anyone moves our way. Bruce and I will sneak over to cabin four and grab Carlotta. We'll run back through the cane field to the van. Rocky's the driver."

He looked at Rocky. "Be ready to drive like hell when we get back."

"Sounds good." Let's go get her."

Everyone nodded. We held our fists out, touched, and moved out. Greg and Benny zoomed out. Cap and I slouched down as we ran towards the cabin. I was in the lead and heard a thud, then a sharp bleating behind me. I stopped and looked around to see that Cap had tripped and fallen over a goat that was squirming to stand up. Cap looked up at me and whispered "Sorry, I ran into her, I couldn't see anything."

I waited until the goat trotted away. Cap stood up and whispered "Let's go."

We walked onward. The darn goat was following Cap. We reached the front porch of the fourth cabin. The door swung open with a slight squeak. Greg was smiling as he held the door open. He pointed at Carlotta sleeping next to the wall. We tip toed past the other sleepers. Their breathing was louder than our steps. I put my hand over her mouth and tapped her on the shoulder. She woke up instantly. I could see the whites of her eyes looking up at me. I put my finger over my mouth to signal her to be quiet, and lifted her up, and carried her out of the cabin. Although she had no clue we were coming, once we were outside she "followed the script" and ran behind us into the cane field. We slowed down, but still made noise stepping on the canes. I stopped and held my hand in the air. That didn't do much good as we bumped into each other, Carlotta hitting me, Cap hitting her and I'm not sure what you call it when ghosts walk into you because Greg smiled. I looked out at the veranda and saw the man stand up looking our way. Benny was standing next to him and whispered "It's those damn deer." He seemed to blow the words into his ear. Well, it worked, as the guard sat down unalarmed and closed his eyes.

Chapter 53

12:00 PM, Noon

"She hasn't spoken all morning," I told Rocky.

"Where is she?"

"She's soaking in the bath tub."

"There are no bruises or scratches on her body," said Benny from the end of the sofa.

"Hey, that's not fair. You shouldn't be looking at my wife naked."

"Can't help it. It's one of the benefits of being a spirit," he grinned.

"Geez. Can't wait 'til I'm a ghost." I sarcastically stated.

The bathroom door opened. The tub was gurgling as the water drained out. Carlotta stepped out with a towel wrapped around her and said, "I want to get my hair done. Where are the car keys?"

"I pulled them out of my pocket and set them on the table.

She picked the keys up and walked into the bedroom to dress. A few minutes later I heard the back door close and the car back out.

237

After she left, Benny said, "She needs time alone to adjust."

I brought two Abita Ambers out of the fridge and handed one to Rocky and Cap Black. I shook my head at Benny and said "You don't drink anymore."

"Very funny. I could die for a drink. God, I miss it. Remember that time we got caught drinking beer in the dorm?"

"Yeah," I said. "We had cans of beer hidden in the laundry bag and the hall monitor heard the empty cans clinking."

Benny said, "It's easy to laugh now. But, now, as I look back. I died from drinking. I drank too much. It killed my liver." He looked down and pinched his stomach where his liver used to be.

Rocky looked at me above his glasses. "You worry me. You really need help. Talking to ghosts is crazy, far out."

Cap Black smiled as he sipped his beer.

***

2:00 PM

Carlotta came back from getting her hair done and set the keys on the counter. She looked like a different woman. Her hair was dyed blue, short and curly.

"How do you like it?" she asked.

"Arggggh…" I cleared my throat. "I's different. It's cute."

"That's what I wanted. To look more like the way I feel."

She went in the kitchen and came back clutching a big carrot.

I looked at her and said, "Please sit down so we can talk."

"I'm not used to sitting. We weren't allowed to sit. At least during the day time we couldn't sit. We either stood or stooped, mostly. Walked to get somewhere and that was it."

"Well, now you can relax. Sit down."

She remained standing, so I asked "Tell me what happened. How did you get there?"

She looked at me for a long time. I stared back and waited. She wet her lips, then pursed them tightly together before saying, "After I left the house, I was on Frenchman Street watching a brass band play on the corner. The two guys next to me were smoking weed. It smelled funny. They were giggling. They saw me watching them and offered me a smoke. I inhaled and liked it, so I inhaled again. The guy that handed it to me said, 'Hey, you can keep that one, we got plenty more.'"

"I've never seen you smoke before."

"Well, I had a second one later while sitting under that big tree on the neutral ground by Check Point Charlies."

"That's where the gutter punks hang out."

"Well, I fell asleep there. I don't know how long I was sleeping when I heard squad cars pull up. I didn't hear any sirens. I held my hands over my eyes because of the bright flashing blue lights. A police officer jerked me up by the arm forcing me to my feet. He put cuffs on me, walked me to the police car, put his hand on my head and pushed me in. It was like a bad dream. I was so groggy, I couldn't talk.

More police cars came. "They picked up everyone that was too tired, stoned, or drunk to run. They didn't say where we were going. We thought we were going to the police station. Whenever I'd ask a question, I was told to shut up.

"They drove us out into the country. It was the middle of the night. They dropped us off at an old plantation. Well, you saw it. We were drowsy from smoking weed and didn't resist. They led us into the small shacks. I just wanted to sleep.

"I woke up the next morning to loud shouting outside. A man dressed in black was screaming at us to wake up. Seconds later, he kicked the door slamming it against the wall. He grabbed the first person and pushed him outside. Then he grabbed the next person and the others stumbled out on their own until we all stood outside. He went through the other cabins and did the same thing until everyone was outside. There were more people than I thought, around thirty. The man in black and three other men led us to a shed where they sprayed all of us with a hose. We were told to remove our wet clothes and put on dry clothes lying on a table. Then, we were marched over to a long table and given a bowl and spoon. A woman ladled grits into our bowl and gave us a hard biscuit. There were no chairs, so we stood eating. When we finished, we were led to an outhouse. Thank God there were two – one for women and one for men. We were then led back to our shacks and found them empty. All our personal belongings were gone."

I listened to her talk nonstop for hours. Since she was not allowed to talk at the planation, she was bursting with words. The more she spoke, the more I listened. It was the most incredible story that I had ever heard. Their identities were stolen physically and mentally. It was as though their lives up until then were erased and they were starting completely over.

"The man in black called us outside the cabins. We stood in line, shoulder to shoulder, in front of each cabin. The man said we had to call him Master, and speak only when spoken to, and never to each other. He said whenever we hear the big bell ring we were to stand at attention and listen to orders.

"He told us that we would be given jobs based on our skills. One of his men, who we were told to address as Captain, shouted out, "COOKS! IF YOU CAN COOK, WALK OVER HERE. Then he

241

shouted out for carpenters, painters, cleaners, farmers and gardeners to form separate groups. He told the remaining people to stay put."

"Why didn't you escape? Couldn't you run away? I didn't see any fence?"

"The first day I begged him to let me go. I told them that it was a mistake. That I didn't belong with these people. I had a life. I had a husband. That I should go home to my husband who'll be looking for me. He didn't believe me. He said he heard it before. It's all lies. He said if I tried to leave I would be whipped.

"Later that week one of the young boys was tied to a stake and whipped for trying to run away. We were all made to watch the whipping. His back was raw. It was awful. His back was lined with blood. No one tried to escape after that night.

"It seemed that a police van pulled up once or twice a week to drop off people. They were blended into the different work groups. The gardens were constantly expanded to grow more food. The main house was repaired and painted. There was constant pounding and sawing as more shacks were built. The young men worked in the fields all day. I guess the reason was to tire them out, because when they came back at night, they could hardly walk. They usually fell asleep until the next day. I was a cook and when I wasn't cooking, I worked in the gardens, weeding, planting and harvesting vegetables.

If they didn't think we were working hard enough, they would yell at us. We never got used to it. They worked us so hard that we were always tired and hungry. Our only time off was on Sunday afternoons, and we were too exhausted to do anything but rest."

"Who were these people? Were they criminals or what?"

"They were hitch hikers, train hoppers, gutter punks, bums, homeless by choice, some of them had fallen on hard times, others just had nothing and some were criminals. The common denominator was that most of them didn't have jobs. Some had bank accounts, some begged and mooched, some robbed and stole. They did whatever it took to exist."

She added, "Word got around that New Orleans was easy. That the police were lax and didn't bother you. There was plenty of easy money to be had from tourists. They just had to ask for it or take it. Vagrancy is not illegal in New Orleans. The word was the police are handicapped by laws that are too lenient."

"So why did the police change? Why were you and the others picked up?"

"I don't know. Maybe, club owners, shop owners, tourists complained enough to the point where the vagrancy was too much."

"So you were taken because the police thought you were one of them. What happened?"

"What I heard is that one of the shop owners complained about the gutter punks partying all day and night. Someone threw a bottle through a shop window and the owner was fed up and called the police."

"Yeah, but you never hung out with them before."

"I met some people who offered me weed. I had never smoked it and was curious to see what it was like smoking a couple. I got a little carried away, started to feel drowsy, couldn't walk, and fell asleep. I woke up when I heard screaming and saw flashing blue lights. The police were grabbing the people next to me pulling them up and shoving them into the squad cars. I woke up really groggy and literally got thrown into the police van. I couldn't talk because I was so hung over from smoking weed. My body wasn't used to it."

Carlotta and I talked until the wee hours of the morning. At least it seemed like it since we both fell asleep where we were sitting in the living room. I was glad she was back. Nothing else mattered.

I was used to living alone – almost. But, I will be forever grateful to my friends and especially Rocky, Greg, Benny and Cap because without them I never would've found her and I know I never would've survived getting killed.

I wondered how she really felt inside. Was she happy to be home or did she like her life on the plantation?

***

Rain started pelting the windows. When it rains in New Orleans, it pours buckets. I liked the rain because of its power and might. It did an excellent job of cleaning. It washed the dust and litter off the sidewalks and streets. The smell of the rain was almost intoxicating. People would open their windows and doors to inhale the fresh air after a rain. It smelled sweet. Ooh. Suddenly, I felt a cold draft.

"Well, I don't like it at all. Rain gives me the chills," said Greg, who appeared on the sofa across from me.

"How can it give you the chills?" You're a ghost. You don't have a body?" I asked.

He blinked several times and scratched his beard and said, "Water makes me feel cold. Rain hits me sharply like shots from the Doctor, only it pricks me all over and goes through me. It hurts."

"What's it like being a ghost? Were you a ghost right away after you passed? Or did you have to wait a while?"

Greg looked at me. His eyes looked different than when he was alive. Now they seemed to stare longer and hold steadier when he looked at you.

"I don't know how to describe it. It feels strange, but good. I'm not used to it yet. I don't know what the limits are. Not sure what I can or cannot do. I

245

just think and appear where I want to, but it feels better to appear where I can help or be a friend to someone. You were a good friend. I feel good being with you."

"Thank you, Greg. I wouldn't be alive today if it weren't for you."

Greg's eyes swelled up, and I saw a tear drop fall out of his left eye before he vanished.

"Who are you talking to?" Carlotta asked as she walked out of the bedroom stretching her arms in the air, yawning. "I heard you talking to someone. Who's here?"

Chapter 54

7:00 AM, Saturday, September 6th

I felt a cool draft in the living room. *I thought Greg or Benny must be here.* Since I didn't see Greg or Benny, I walked around to check the windows to see if they were open, but they were all closed. Carlotta was sleeping in the bedroom. I closed the door to let her sleep. I almost sat in my chair, but then decided on the sofa to save the chair for Greg or Benny if they decided to pop in. I turned on my cell phone to check email and the weather forecast and then played scrabble. I gave up when I couldn't spell the capital of North Korea. I put the phone down and laid my head back. My mind drifted as I thought about the past eight months.

***

"It's time for us to walk."

I jerked my head up to see Greg standing in front of me.

"A walk? I don't wanna leave Carlotta.

247

"It won't take long." Greg looked serious.

"Where to?"

"Come. Come with me." Greg looked different. He was translucent. He held his hand out for me and opened the door.

***

We went to the St. Louis cemetery No. 1 on Basin Street. The main entrance was chain locked, so we walked through the maintenance gate. Greg was still in the lead as we walked slowly between tombs. The tombs are above ground because of the high water level in New Orleans. We finally stopped in front of a white marble tomb with fresh flowers and a small spruce tree in a pot in front of it. The name of the deceased was engraved in large Roman capital letters. It read

"BRUCE PAUL

DIED JULY 9, 2019."

I looked at Greg and shook my head. "No. No. That's crazy, I'm not dead. Today's September 6th. This is a bad dream"

He looked at me and said softly, "Bruce, it's OK. You found Carlotta. You brought her home. She's safe. You can rest now. It's OK."

"Are you nuts? What's going on? I'm not dead. No. No. This is wrong. I wanna wake up. Please stop this."

"Bruce, you were killed so you couldn't testify as the key witness in the Barracks Street murder trial. When the thugs beat you up on the street, you died."

"No, no, no. You're joking, right? Come on. Quit this talk. This is a bad joke."

Greg grabbed my arm and led me into the tomb. Somehow we passed through the thick concrete walls. I saw myself lying in a casket. My eyes and mouth were closed. I felt a cold draft as I looked at myself, despite no windows in the tomb. I felt very cold. The coldest I had ever felt. I crossed my arms on my chest and blew out streams of cold air.

"I don't understand. How could I have been going for walks, drinking beer, talking to you, searching for Carlotta, testifying in court, talking to Rocky? Cap Black? How do you explain all that?"

Greg reached out his hand, "Bruce, come with me." I followed him over a gravel path to another tomb. It was gray and a much older tomb with Italian designs on it. There were several names engraved on it. The most recent one read:

"ROCKY MATASSA

DIED JULY 9, 2019"

"Rocky was killed trying to save you. He saw the thugs grab you. He chased them in his taxi van. They shot him six times. He died the same day as you."

I started crying. I couldn't believe it. "It just doesn't make sense. It doesn't make sense. I wanna go home. Please, please take me home. Please."

***

I don't know how much time elapsed, but I "woke up" sitting on the sofa in my house. Greg was sitting in my chair staring at me.

I felt empty. Hollow inside. I rubbed my eyes. "I have a question, is Carlotta alive or dead? Is she a ghost too?"

"She's alive. You saved her."

"But, she saw me. How could she see me?"

"She saw you because of your deep love for her. It was important for you to find her and bring her back. It was your mission. Now that she's back and is safe, it's time for you to go."

"Go where?"

"To rest. You are now like me, Rocky, and Benny."

I started crying. Tears were streaming down my cheeks. "Will she see me when she wakes up?"

"Do you want her to see you?"

Chapter 55

9:00 AM, Saturday

Sunlight was leaking through the wood shutters. I woke up on the sofa and walked into the bedroom to check on Carlotta. The creaking of the hardwood floors betrayed my presence as she stirred when I entered the room. She turned over and smiled at me. I bent down to kiss her. She sat up and wrapped her arms around my neck. I put my arms around her and lifted her up out of bed. I didn't want to let go and held her tightly.

"I love you, I love you, I love you," I said.

"I love you, too." She said. We kissed and held each other as if we really would never let go.

CHAPTER 56

11:30 PM, Saturday

"FOLLOW ME!" Cap Black yelled, waving a long black flashlight in the air, as he led fifty people from St. Benedict's church in New Orleans' seventh ward. People lined up in single file to board four old yellow school buses. After everyone was on board, Cap jumped in to drive the lead bus. Singing erupted on the buses. "We shall overcome. We shall overcome!" could be heard loudly as windows were opened.

It was eleven o'clock at night. Cap had recruited as many people as possible to help him overtake Jacque Landry and his men at the planation prison. He told the people about the deplorable life and abuse that was going on at the plantation. After he explained that "slavery" was going on, the crowd buzzed with energy as they boarded the buses.

Yes, they were certainly high on energy but low on weapons. Cap didn't believe in violence or guns, and he made that clear to everyone.

The plan was to park the buses in front of the house and move out orderly, then rush Landry and his men in the plantation house. Cap handed out rope and flashlights as people stepped off the buses.

"Tie their hands behind their backs and sit them down on the porch," he ordered.

***

Carlotta and Bruce were sleeping in their house. Well the truth is that Bruce had been unconscious for three days and nights. He had fallen asleep that first night with Carlotta and never woke up. He appeared to be in a coma. The Doctor said he'd never seen anything like it. Bruce's breathing was normal. Lab tests showed that he was healthy. The Doctor was puzzled and said that perhaps it was the shock to his system from the emotional stress that he had experienced during the past twelve months with Carlotta missing and witnessing the two murders.

***

After the Doctor left their house that night, Cap summoned Madam Sherry to help. He explained to her that Bruce was comatose. She hurried over to his house and stood over Bruce. She knelt down, prayed in cryptic words and rubbed his forehead

254

and cheeks with oil. She felt his arms, shoulders, and legs. "He's cold. Very cold. Bring me towels and hot water."

While she was waiting, she reached in her bag and took out nine deep red candles, a feather pen and an ink bottle. She looked at Carlotta and ordered her to write "Bruce" three times on each candle. After the candles were ascribed, Madam Sherry washed each candle with Van Van (an old hoodoo formula for oil, incense, sachet powders, and washing products designed to clear away evil and provide magical protection). She lit each candle with wood matches from her bag and handed the first candle to Carlotta and seven others to the people in the room.

Holding a lit candle up Madam Sherry looked above it. "Bruce. Bruce. Bruce. Return to us. Almighty God. We pray to you to bring Bruce's spirit back to his body so that he may live."

Carlotta was sobbing. Others in the room joined in chanting "Bruce, Bruce. Bruce. Return to us."

A lady handed Madam Sherry a bowl of hot water and a folded towel. She dipped it in the hot water and rubbed his body from head to foot to warm him up.

"His spirit is gone." She looked around the bedroom and pointed at Greg and Benny, "You. Go find his spirit now! Hurry! You gotta find it before it's too late!"

Madam Sherry knelt down again and prayed over Bruce, saying words that only she knew what they meant.

***

Meanwhile, Cap Black led the charge out of the buses onto the Landry plantation. They quickly overcame a guard sleeping on the porch. Four men held him, while his arms were being tied behind his back.

***

Greg and Benny were literally gliding in the wind searching for Bruce's spirit all over the plantation grounds. They stopped when they saw Cap and his army storm the house.

***

Carlotta was crying again. She felt so helpless and guilty because Bruce had saved her and brought her home and now was lifeless. He meant everything to her.

Madam Sherry hugged her and told her that it would be alright. "Greg and Benny will find his spirit."

***

Cap Black was unstoppable. He and his men stormed up the stairs to the master bedroom and pounced on Landry lying in bed with his wife. "HURRY," Cap shouted as he flipped Landry over and forced his arms behind his back as another man wound a rope around him. (Before Landry could reach for his pistol in the holster hanging on the bed post.) Cap told Landry's wife to stay in bed, and she wouldn't be harmed.

Two men held Landry's arms and walked him down the stairway to the front porch where they tied him to the railing. Next, Cap and his men checked the other bedrooms. They captured four men, bound them, and walked them down stairs.

Then Cap ordered the volunteer army standing in front of the house to free the people from the shacks and work buildings.

***

At seven thirty in the morning, Madam Sherry knocked on the front door and let herself in. This time she carried a larger handbag.

"Good morning," she held her hand out to Carlotta.

"Thank you for coming so early, Madam Sherry."

257

She walked directly to the bedroom and without explanation, Madam Sherry opened her bag and emptied its contents on the bed.

***

It seemed that Cap Black's 'army' had swelled to more than two hundred as the freed workers blended in with the volunteers. Cap stood on the plantation porch addressing them, "You workers who were captive here, are free now. Go board the buses for New Orleans."

Many of them looked at each other not knowing what to do. Everything happened so fast. Suddenly, someone clapped, then another and another, and finally the whole crowd erupted, clapping and cheering.

Cap smiled, nodded, and held his hands high in the air, acknowledging their cheers. "This is all about you. It's not about me. It's about people, helping people. You can thank me and all these good people who volunteered to free you by going back and help other people."

As people filed into the buses, Cap wondered if Bruce was living or dead. He didn't realize that Greg and Benny were also at the plantation searching for Bruce's spirit.

***

Madam Sherry sprinkled red rose petals on Bruce's body. Then she spread ashes on top of the rose petals. She placed chicken legs, crawfish and alligator parts on him. Carlotta and others were watching intently. When she was done using up the contents of her bag, she set it on the floor, and knelt over Bruce. She held his right hand and chanted in a foreign tongue. Madam Sherry wasn't aware that Greg and Benny were standing behind her and Carlotta. They had returned from their search, but didn't want to interrupt Madam Sherry's chant.

***

Cap Black and his swelled "army" of one hundred twenty were laughing and singing on the drive back to New Orleans. Cap could feel the love in the air as both the volunteers and the freed captives were happy and thankful. The energy level was off the charts. He thought about Bruce as he drove, and hoped he was OK. He whispered to himself "God help Bruce. Please let him live."

***

Carlotta broke out crying while Madam Sherry was praying over Bruce's body. She reached over to hold Carlotta's hand with her free hand. She still held on firmly to Bruce's hand.

259

Suddenly, she felt a warm sensation, a tingling, in both hands. She opened her eyes and looked at Bruce and saw his eye lids quivering slightly as if he was in a dream state. Carlotta noticed it, too.

Madam Sherry's back was jolted by the surging energy. She felt it going through her body as she continued holding both Bruce's and Carlotta's hands.

When she saw Bruce blinking his eyes, Carlotta stopped crying and erupted, "OH, OH MY GOD!" Benny and Greg stood next to them smiling because they had found Bruce's spirit and combined with the power of Madam Sherry had brought it back to his body. They both faded away, turning gray and then transparent as Bruce came back to life. He opened his eyes completely and said in a hoarse voice, "Where am I?"

Madam Sherry leaned over and said, "You're home dear. You're home!" Carlotta sobbed uncontrollably as she knelt down and kissed Bruce over and over with her tears dropping on his face.

THE END

Epilogue

Earlier that night, Rocky and Cap Black stood in the bedroom doorway watching Bruce lying in bed. They were hoping for a miracle. It was dark in the room except for several candles. They raised their heads when they heard a strange buzz and saw a cloud or swarm of light flickering in the air drifting lower towards Bruce's body.

Outside Bruce's window were several hundred people holding candles.

Cap had told the volunteers and freed captives, earlier, when they were gathered at St. Bernard's, that they were all heroes. He urged them to pay it forward. "Do well. Help others. Love one another other. We're all family.

"There's one hero who's not here tonight. His name is Bruce Paul. He's in a coma. He's fighting for his life. His spirit left him. He's the reason I'm here."

He went on to tell them about Bruce's relentless search and undying love for his wife, Carlotta. Cap raised his voice and said, "This man never gave up. He found her, and he found you!"

He paused as his voice began breaking up, "I'm walking over to his house now."

When Cap walked out of St. Bernard's, without being told, everyone followed him. When they reached Bruce's house, the crowd stood silent outside holding candles. The night seemed timeless. Although there had been no wind, suddenly a breeze, in the form of a cloud, absorbed the light from their candles, and drifted toward the house. A hush came over the crowd as the "light cloud" seemed to go through the side of the house.

Inside something special was happening. The energy from the cloud entered Bruce's body.

A few minutes later, Cap opened the front door and shouted "BRUCE ISN'T DEAD! HE'S ALIVE! HE'S ALIVE!"

ODE TO CARLOTTA

CARLOTTA, CARLOTTA!
LET'S DANCE THE NIGHT AWAY.
CARLOTTA, CARLOTTA!
YOU ALWAYS SEEM TO GET AWAY.

CARLOTTA, CARLOTTA!
WHY DO YOU HAVE TO GO?
CARLOTTA, OH CARLOTTA!
YOU'RE ALWAYS RUNNING OUT THE DOOR!

CARLOTTA, CARLOTTA!
YOU LOVE TO WALK TO FRENCHMAN
STREET,
TO SHAKE YOUR ARMS AND DANCE YOUR
FEET.
CARLOTTA, CARLOTTA,

WON'T YOU STAY HOME WITH ME?
CARLOTTA, OH CARLOTTA,
YOU GOTTA RUN SO FREE.
CARLOTTA, CARLOTTA,

PLEASE COME BACK TO ME,
SO WE CAN LIVE HAPPILY.
CARLOTTA, CARLOTTA!
PLEASE COME BACK TO ME,
SO WE CAN LIVE HAPPILY.

Author's Note

The orginal idea for this book was to write about the fascinating culture and social dynamics of New Orleans. Living in this city is like living in a pot of Gumbo because of its diversity. Nowhere else is there such a great mix of smells, flavors, sounds, people, and laughter. I'd be remiss if I didn't mention that its people love to celebrate and have fun. They invite everyone to embrace it like they do by experiencing its historic sites, colorful parades, streetcars, Creole and Cajun restaurants , incredible music (inside clubs and outside on street corners), riverboats, plantations, City Park with the world's largest collection of hundreds of years old live oak trees, aligators in nearby bayous, Voodoo, mediums and card readers and yes even ghosts.

Every day offers opportunities for new adventures and experiences. Life is a journey that we all endeavor when we wake up each day. Cracked Sidewalks is about good and bad experiences that occur, sometimes unexpectedly, and how important it is to have friends (living and not living) to help us survive our journey.

I hope you enjoyed the book. Peace and Love.

jbsensen@gmail.com

265

Made in the USA
Columbia, SC
29 October 2023